The Invasion Series

Book One

RESISTANCE

by

J.F. Holmes

Dedicated to all the men and women of my fan group, Irregular Scout Team One. Without your immeasurable feedback, this book would never have happened. You're a bunch of obnoxious jerks, but I love you all anyway.

Except you. You annoy the crap out of me. You know who you are.

~ FOB Stillwater, ZA year 5

Make sure you check out all the adventures of Irregular Scout Team One and my other books!

and join the guys in the Team Room!

Prologue

Somewhere in the ruins of North America

He couldn't really call it a war, because the enemy couldn't know that he was there. If the intrusion was discovered, death would be instantaneous. Still, he patiently navigated his way through traps and blinds, gathered knowledge, and left small distractions and traps of his own. Learning, mapping, waiting.

Waiting for the call to come. Waiting to strike.

Upstate New York

"Listen," said the man, adjusting the green armband on his uniform sleeve, looking across the table at the other person "what you're doing is extremely important. We need to work with them, they're the future of the Earth. You're young; how old were you when the Invy came?"

"Eight," came the answer, a bit louder to speak over the rising roar of an Invy shuttlecraft, just outside the window.

"Then you don't really remember how bad the pollution and environmental damage was. I grew up by the Hudson River, and it's going to be another hundred years before we can eat any fish from there. The Invy are the best thing that ever happened to us."

There was no answer; his infiltrator was contemplating the enormity of what they were being asked to do. After a minute, the question came. "Do you really think there's an organized resistance to the Invy? There's been no attacks, no warfare. It's been quiet since the actual invasion."

The man with the armband had an answer to that. "That's why I suspect there is. It's been TOO quiet. Human nature insists on resistance to impingement of their freedoms, and it's unnatural. Someone, somewhere, is ordering what was left of the military to bide their time. The fact that the Invy refuse to believe that humanity is capable of such a thing, well, they have their blind spots. Arrogance is one."

"And you want me to find out? What then?"

The collaborator said, "Then you use the brains that God gave you and play the situation from there. Get the information, and get back to me, if you can. Go as high up as you can. If not, then strike when the opportunity arises."

"And when I get back with this information, we'll go to the Invy with it?"

"Yes, and hopefully they'll believe us then."

Far South Atlantic

The CEF submarine *Knyaz Pozharskiy* was in trouble, and her captain knew it. Unless they got the reactor back on line within the next five minutes, they were screwed. The backup diesels had given up the ghost last year; it was the reason they were headed to the Azores Base for a refit.

He drove the engineering section hard, but there was nothing they could do. The reactor controls had a fault somewhere, and they would need days to figure it out. Meanwhile, the ship wallowed in the troughs of the South Atlantic waves, rocking from side to side.

Looking at his watch, he ordered his men to abandon ship. They scrambled to the rafts; as each one was placed over the side, a team of pilot whales guided and pulled them northwest towards the CEF base at Tierra del Fuego. He wasn't too worried about blowing the CEF's cover; the Invy had killed more than two dozen submarines in the years since the invasion. None had brought any more scrutiny.

Damn arrogant sons of bitches, just because they held the high ground.

"Well," he said out loud, "*Krasnaya Zarya* will show them."

"Da, Captain," answered his XO. "I only wish we could have been there to participate." Both knew that there wasn't time to get away from the incoming orbital strike. Any manmade object of that size on the open ocean was sure to get hit.

There were still a dozen crewmen aboard when the Invy orbital crested the horizon, a pinpoint of light moving across the northern sky. With a half forgotten prayer, the Captain ordered the last of his men to take to the water, despite the bone chilling cold. Then he stood on the bridge and watched as a spark appeared and grew slowly brighter.

"Damn you to hell, you bastards!" he managed to scream, before the tungsten rod, dropped from Low Earth Orbit, impacted amidships. The *Borie* class submarine shattered, the missiles onboard detonating in a thunderous roar, killing every sailor in the water who hadn't frozen to death already, and flipping the rafts that had started to be towed away.

No survivors ever made it back to the CEF base, and the fleet was down to seven.

Part One

July 2047, Eleven Years Post-Invasion, formerly Upstate New York

Chapter One

Energy weapons crackled past as they hustled through the main cavern into a side tunnel, the invaders firing low, disciplined bursts. A bolt slammed into the wall next to him, and General Warren cried out in pain, molten stone splattering his face. He fired with his pistol until the slide locked back, empty, not sure if he'd hit anything in the flickering darkness.

Beside him, the Special Forces (Delta) operator, last of his bodyguard, yelled, "GO, KID! GET THE HELL OUT OF HERE!" and turned, firing his M-6 carbine back at the advancing figures. The sergeant cursed, damning all the aliens to hell as his weapon was shattered by a plasma bolt, mangling his arm. With his uninjured hand, he shoved the teenaged General toward the yawning door, pushing him backward.

The last David Warren had seen of him as the door slammed shut, the soldier was whipping out a long combat knife and charging forward. With a quiet snick the door closed off, sealing the General in blackness as the ground shook from the orbital strikes.

"Uncle, wake up!"

David groaned, but the shaking didn't stop. He sat up suddenly with a yell, reaching for a non-existent pistol, and Jeremy stepped back from him. He knew that, in the grip of a nightmare, his uncle could lash out unexpectedly.

"Ugh, sorry Jeremy. Was it bad this time?" he said, wiping his face with his hand.

"Mom heard you yelling orders and told me to wake you up. Who is Kira?"

David shook his head. "Nobody. A name from the past. She's dead now." He rolled over and sat on the edge of the bed, holding up his hand to quiet his nephew. The boy, a gangly teenager, didn't remember much from eleven years ago, and he quizzed his uncle constantly, much to the older man's annoyance.

"I'll be down in a minute. What's on the agenda today?"

The kid was already making his way down the stairs; he had chores to do. He called back over his shoulder, "Gotta hitch up the horses and pull that stump."

"Shit," Warren muttered under his breath, and started washing his face in the basin. The dawn light coming in through the window caught his features, and the reflection in the cracked mirror startled him. Burn scars stood out pale on his cheek, in sharp contrast to skin tanned from working outside. "When the hell did I start going gray? I'm only twenty-eight." His reflection didn't answer him, but he knew that the war had left more than physical scars on him. It was a wonder that it wasn't all gray. A decent razor would be nice, too.

He rubbed at his beard, wondering if they should go on a recovery expedition to one of the ruined towns. Maybe poke around a Walmart, see if there was anything left. Or, they could go trade in Syracuse.

No, not that, he thought. It was an Invy town, like all towns were. Not yet. Not even after more than a decade. He put his thoughts aside and struggled into his threadbare jeans, hip aching from another old wound.

"DAVID! GET IT WHILE IT'S HOT!" his sister yelled up the stairs. Sighing and wishing for toothpaste, he walked stiffly down.

"Hey, can I get some orange juice and bacon to go with these eggs?" he asked, and Victoria gave him a dirty look.

"How about you just take your ass to Denny's and harass the waitress there?" she shot back, but grinned a bit anyway. "This isn't some damn restaurant."

"Oatmeal it is then, don't want to piss off the lady of the house."

"So," said his nephew, "we're running kinda low on nails for the horses. Could use some metal for shoes, too."

"Take some corn over in trade to Zoe's place. I know we can't spare it, but the horses have to be shoed. Roads are getting worse."

The teen hesitated, and then said what had been on David's mind in the first place. "Maybe we could go to Cazenovia and check around the edges of the crater, see if there's anything left in any of the buildings that we could trade."

Victoria looked at him, a cold, cold look, and her son turned away. "I guess not," he muttered, pushed his plate away, and said, "I'll be out in the barn."

"You know you can't keep him here forever," David told his sister. She was twelve years older than him, and had been raising her toddler son when the Invy came. He had found them after the first long, horrible winter, and taken over the job of her missing husband, becoming like a father to the boy. Still, he always yielded to her when they disagreed. Jeremy wasn't his son, after all.

"I know," she answered. Her blonde hair was streaked with gray, and lines of worry and her own scars reminded him of just how much they had suffered. "I just, well, you know how he worships you. The big general, the war hero. I don't want him doing something rash to try and prove himself to you."

"Victoria, I'm no hero. We lost. It's over. He knows that."

Her face flashed with sudden anger. "Does he? I've heard the stories you tell him. About your friends, about how tight you all were." Her knuckles turned white as she closed her hands around the mug of precious tea, and for a moment he thought she was going to throw it at him. She was right, though. Sometimes, on the frigid winter nights, or while working together out in the fields, he did slip, reminiscing. "I just miss them, sometimes."

She shot back bitterly, "And I don't miss my husband? Or my job? Or my daughter?" Silent tears were streaming down her face.

David Warren, former General of the Combined Earth Forces, stood and placed his hand on his sister's shoulder. It was an old argument, one they'd had even more frequently as her son had grown. "I'm sorry," he said. "I'm sorry I wasn't good enough. I won't let him down." She nodded and wiped her at her tears, then turned her back to him.

He stepped out onto the porch as the sun rose over a ridge to the east, and he watched as an Invy shuttle rose from the ruins of Syracuse, thirty miles away, a silver spark glinting in the light of a new day.

Bastards.

Chapter 2

He heard the horses long before he saw them, and called to Jeremy to join him out by the road. Then he stuck his head back in the door. "Victoria," he called, "travelers!"

People passing through were usually a good source of news; one they looked forward to, but with caution. David grabbed the AK-74 that was hung in the mudroom, making sure the magazine was seated properly and slipping several more into his pockets. His sister came out cradling a 12 gauge pump in her arms, but said nothing; still angry at him, she just walked past. He sighed and followed her out. She'd get over it soon enough.

By the time they had walked the hundred yards down the dirt driveway, Jeremy was already ahead of them, talking to the man and woman who had dismounted from their horses. David noted the eagerness that was on his nephew's face, and thought back to when he was fifteen, at the start of Project Brightstar. Social media had been all the rage, and he had been in contact with people around the world, discussing the construction of the fleet and the unification. Now, at fifteen, Jeremy had to walk more than three miles down the road to find anyone his own age.

No rifles or other long guns, but that was a given. Invy travel rules forbade it, and limited parties to three people only, unless on an escorted trading caravan. Then you ran the risk of becoming the random dinner of one of their troops. Still, the man openly wore a .45 strapped to his leg, and the woman had what looked like a small submachine gun slung around her in a tactical rig. Small enough that it would appear as a pistol to passing Wolverine patrols, but an edge in a fight. His implant immediately identified it as a Neal .22 caliber, fifty shot with a rate of fire of fifty rounds per second. A World War Two design that had never actually been manufactured, and his suspicions jumped into high gear.

The man was white, burly and unshaven, a long "veterans" beard obscuring his facial features, and a floppy desert camo pattern hat. The woman was small, brown skinned, with distinct Indian features. She wore a tattered Yankees ball cap that she kept low over her eyes, and didn't look him in the eye, making it hard to see her face.

"Morning!" David said as they came up, moving the AK's selector lever from SAFE to AUTO, with an exaggerated gesture that they both noted. "What's the news?"

"I'm Nick, and this is my wife, Rachel. We're passing through, maybe looking for work. Heard there's a trading caravan going from Syracuse to Albany, maybe we can hire out our horses as pack animals. We ain't had much to eat lately, crop failed."

"Sure, we can give you something to tide you over to 'cuse" interjected Jeremy before his uncle could say anything. "It's only about another thirty miles. Did you see any Invy on the way here? There's a patrol that goes by once a week or so, up Route 20."

"Jeremy, why don't you get to the barn and see if anyone might be working their way back there, intent on stealing while we talk to these people? You know the drill."

The teen's face wilted, but he shouldered his own shotgun, and sauntered off. There was no real danger of thieves, but it would keep him occupied.

"Now," said Victoria, in a pleasant tone that belied the lack of a smile on her face, "where did you say you were coming from?"

"We didn't, yet," answered the woman, her dark hair and dusky skin set off by green eyes, "but we came up 81 from outside Binghamton. Had a place there, but like Nick said, our corn got hit with some kind of bug; we lost it all last week." Her voice had a musical, accented lilt to it.

The man who called himself Nick said nothing as his wife talked with Victoria, just looked intently at David, then said, "Ever been down to Binghamton? You look really familiar."

The question was unexpected, and a chill ran up and down the former General's spine. "No," he quickly answered, "I was just starting college when the orbital strikes began, and we've been here ever since. How about yourself?"

"Lost a leg in the Spratly War, a year before the Invy showed up. Got me this and a purple heart, and I was going to school on the GI Bill when they hit," he answered, rolling his pant leg up to reveal a carbon fiber leg. David saw that, even though he was talking to him, the man's eyes moved from place to place, always scanning the area behind and around them. He noticed that the woman did, also, and she never looked him fully in the face.

"If you two are done dick-measuring, David, we can give them some cornbread and water. I'm sorry," Victoria said to them, "but we don't have any work for you. Come back in September when we're harvesting."

"Fair enough," answered the woman, eyes still scanning.

"David, I'll go get them some food, and you and Jeremy can pump them for all the news they can give." She left without a backwards glance, just as her son came jogging up.

"Don't mind my mom," said the teen. "She just doesn't like to hear about the outside world. Makes her remember too much. But I'm game! Have you seen much? I've never been more than twenty miles from my house since the war, and of course I'm too young to remember much else!"

Nick grinned at this enthusiasm, and sat down on stump, tying off his horse. "Well," he said," if your old man here would put his weapon on safe, we'll give you all the gossip we've heard along the way."

"Not my old man, he's my uncle," said Jeremy.

"That so?" said the woman, who sat down next to her husband. David noted, though, that they sat almost back to back, watching different areas of approach.

"Yep. My dad was killed in the war, don't really remember him."

Rachel's face softened a bit, and she almost smiled, though she still wouldn't look Warren full in the face. "I lost my parents too, I was a little older than you, but still. Just going to college and being oblivious. It's a hard world we live in." He grinned back at her; a pretty woman other than his mother, even a married one, was a rare sight to see.

"Well," said Nick, "we come up from Binghamton after some fools tried to start a town. Did you see the flash?"

"Saw the reentry trail of a thunderbolt about a week and a half ago."

The older man made a show of thinking, then said, "Yeah that would be about right. They figured that, well, it's been over ten years, and they nearest Invy town is up here in Syracuse, so maybe they could get away with it."

"Same old story," said his wife, as Victoria came back up carrying a bag of food and a plastic jug of water. "No more than three on a road, no more than one family group living anywhere. You know the drill."

"That we do. Had a patrol come by two weeks ago and update our pictures." Again the couple exchanged a glance, a quick look that only David caught.

"Ma'am, thank you for the corn bread. We'll be going now," said Nick, and the two untied their horses and mounted. They didn't look back as they headed north, and the three of them watched them go until they were out of sight.

"Hope they find another farm to work, Uncle," said Jeremy. He looked like he wanted to go with them.

His uncle didn't answer for a long minute, then said, "They weren't farmers, J. Not by a long shot."

The beard had prevented his implant from getting a file read on the man's face, and the woman had refused to look him in the eye, and never allowed him to get a full profile. Did they know?

Around the bend, the two horses left the road and started moving cross country, going easily through the overgrown fields. They reached a ruined farm house, went around and into a rickety barn. A burly, bald headed man in a leather bikers' vest slid the door shut behind them; it moved easily in its tracks, belying its weathered look.

He helped Nick down from his horse as Rachel slid off hers. The amputee walked over to a laptop, mated up a smaller unit, and the screen sprang to life, revealing a picture of David Warren, standing in the drive to his house, as they'd last seen him.

"Is that him, Colonel?" asked the Doc Hamilton, the team's second in command. Rachel walked over to the laptop and looked for a long minute.

The Indian woman turned the screen to face him. On it was the first picture, and then another beside it, showing a much younger Warren, wearing a high-necked uniform decorated with five stars on the collar.

Colonel Rachel Singh, Commander, Confederated Earth Forces Scout Regiment, said bitterly, "Rob, that is General David Warren, boy genius of Project Brightstar, and the coward who screwed us all."

Chapter 3

"Listen here, noob," said Sergeant Isiah Jones, unrolling a blanket in front of a starved looking teenager. Night had fallen on the barn, and, rather than getting some shut eye, Jones was explaining their communications equipment to the teenager. "I want you to get to know this shit really well, understand?"

Private Abe Drummond was easing his feet out of his boots, still sore from yesterday's march. He wasn't yet used to the grueling pace that the scouts set. Twenty five miles between sunrise and sunrise, with full packs on their backs, for five days in a row. He was surprised he actually had any legs left.

"Can I ask a question first, Sergeant?" he said, wincing as Doc Hamilton lanced another blister.

"Only dumb question is the one you don't ask," answered Jones.

The younger man put on fresh socks, hoping his boots broke in soon. Growing up in an Invy town outside Scranton, he was used to salvaged sneakers. "How come we don't normally use horses? I mean, I know we have some here, but seems to me they would come in real handy."

"Two reasons. One, you ain't gonna outrun an Invy patrol on a horse. Better to be unseen, let their drones think you're just some poor traveler. Plus, moving at a faster pace, you more often get surprised by them, around a bend in the road or some shit. Then you're getting searched with some military hardware on your ass. Nah, we can see 'em coming easier on foot."

Reaching into his pack, the NCO laid out some more equipment on the blanket. "Second," he continued, "if you have a horse, you tend to pack a lot of shit onto said horse. More than you need, and if you get in a fight and have to dismount, well, all that shit you was countin on, is either skedaddled with the horse, or under a thousand pounds of dead meat. Nah, us scouts gotta carry what we need. Now pay attention."

He held up a pistol shaped object, and walked over to a hole in the barn, consulted a map and compass, aimed in a certain direction, and pulled the trigger. A small diode glowed green, and then went out.

"Coms laser," he told Drummond. "You enter the text on the key board here, and the computer converts it into Morse. Then you aim it at a receiver, in this case one located on an old cell tower here, and it flashes out the signal. Someone with the right set of NVG's can see the scattering light off the receiver, which is really just a bunch of tinfoil or something."

"So I've got to learn to read Morse code?"

"Yep. Is that a problem?" asked the older man.

Drummond blushed in the lamp light, and answered simply, "I don't know how to read, not very much anyway. I learned some in school, before the invasion, but I'm not good at it."

"Well, you gonna learn, then." Jones had seen it often enough; the kids growing under Invy rule were falling further and further behind in their education. Another reason to hate.

"Now, this here is a heliograph. We use it to signal direct to each other when the sun is out. It's good, because it's directional. There's a book of shorthand codes; you'll start learning right away how to read, because information is a scouts' lifeblood."

The NCO went on to describe various arrangements of rocks, branches, and other objects that indicated an information drop was nearby. "Though we don't often leave written stuff just lying in a drop. Mostly it's up here," he said, tapping his dreadlocks.

"You keep messages in your hair?" asked the incredulous Drummond.

Jones scowled and turned to the blonde Corporal who was cleaning her pistols. "Grif, where the hell did you get this kid?"

"A-Team picked him out, sent him to the Scranton recruiter, and he sent him to us. Boy's just pulling your leg, Jay. He ain't as dumb as he looks, and you know we need another man after we lost Carstairs." She flipped blew a stray lock of hair out of her face and said, "He can track, and he can shoot. Plus, he ain't too bad to look at."

"Cradle robber," muttered Jones.

Drummond, to change the embarrassing subject, asked Griffin, "Do I get to go to a base or something, see more cool shit? What's Main Force? Will I go there? Get more training?"

Master Sergeant Agostine said clearly, from where he sat on guard duty above them, "Once you're in the scouts, you're in the scouts till we win, or you die, Drummond. If you desert because you can't take it, two of us will hunt you down and kill you. I've only had to do it to three people, and please don't, we have much more important shit to do."

The young private looked around at the soldiers who were his team mates, trying to decide if it were a joke. They suddenly seemed, well, a bit less friendly and a lot more threatening. He started to wonder what he had gotten himself into.

"I'm good, Master Sergeant. It's just, well, I'm kind of pumped up to know that there really is some fight left, that the CEF still exists. I saw those people in the Invy towns, they seemed so dead." He paused for a second, trying hard to not choke up. "Plus, well, they killed my parents for breaking their stupid rule of three, just stopped to talk to some neighbors they met on the road, and a patrol shot them down, left their bodies to rot in the dirt."

"We all got our sob story, Drummond," came the answer from above. "Just pay attention to Sergeant Jones and make yourself useful."

It was a long night for the young man.

Chapter 4

Master Sergeant Nicholas Agostine stood and stretched, then kicked the blanket next to him, where some black hair peeked out. "Up and at 'em, boss!" Singh groaned, growled a curse, and burrowed deeper into the blankets laid out on the old hay.

At the front of the barn, Sergeant Jones lay full length, watching the northern approach. At the other end, high up in the rafters, PVT Drummond watched to the south. Agostine nodded in satisfaction and woke the rest of the team. When everyone had done their shit, shower and shave, Colonel Singh called the team together. The guards stayed in place, leaving MSG Agostine, SFC Rob "Doc" Hamilton, Staff Sergeant Mike Boyd and Corporal Jen Griffin. They would communicate by heliograph with the sniper team watching the Warren house, Private First Class Tiffany Reynolds and Sergeant Sasha Zivcovic.

"OK, here's the deal. That's him, General Warren. Grif, I want you and Drummond to head back to Scranton, use the Main Force carrier birds to give a heads up to Raven Rock."

"Isn't this important enough to risk a radio?" asked Boyd.

Corporal Griffin, their techie, snorted, a lock of blonde hair falling free. "Even a burst transmission off the ionosphere will get a titanium bar dropped on your head in less than thirty seconds. You know that, you ignorant barbarian."

"I will kill you in your sleep tonight, princess," answered Boyd, with a grin. She gave him the finger in return.

"Can it, you two," said MSG Agostine. He knew that they both owed each other their lives, and neither meant it.

Singh ignored the banter, and gestured for Agostine, the actual team leader, to continue with the tactical decisions. He hunched down and laid out a map. "Ok, you all know that the summer heat messes with the Invy sensors. So we hit them right after the sun goes down, before the heat dissipates. Chameleon suits for the approach. PFC Reynolds and Sergeant Zivcovic will move from overwatch on the house to this highpoint," and he indicated a place on the map, overlooking I-81, "and surveil for Invy patrols."

"Thank God we use the lamp instead of the radio, I can't understand Zivcovic's frigging accent. 'I am from Serbia, I am gangster, and I kill you all in my track suit!'" said Boyd.

"Going to sweat our balls off," called Jones, who never took his attention off the approach.

"Why don't we just snipe him?" asked Doc Hamilton, never one for subtly.

"That's not our mission," answered Singh. "I'm going to talk to him. He's the last survivor of Project Brightstar, and we can use him."

"He's a goddamned traitor, is what he is," said Hamilton, spitting out some tobacco juice. The medic was the only one there, besides Agostine and Singh, who had been in the service when the war ended.

"Be that as it may, he could be useful if the time ever comes to take action. Better to have him come willingly, but there's no reason to kill him. He's got to live with what he did." Agostine continued drawing the approaches to the house in the dirt. They wargamed it for a while, until he was satisfied that everyone understood their roles.

"We move out at twenty hundr-" he was interrupted by a whistle from PVT Drummond, and the team sprang into action. Griffin ran to the horses, and whipped a heavy cloth over them as she spoke a word. They instantly melted into the background, holding stock still. Then she activated the pants she wore, with the same effect, finally pulling a green hoodie over her head, causing the rest of her to disappear.

Another low whistle sounded, and followed by a rattle of bolts being racked back and forward. "Wolverines!" came quietly from where Drummond had disappeared. There was a hissing sound as someone sprayed a scent neutralizer, and then all went quiet.

Outside, the Invy patrol moved down the hill, a standard quad of Wolverines, each moving low to the ground, one tracking, one looking low, another high, the last constantly glancing to the rear.

Rachel Singh watched them closely, amazed at how evolution had paralleled earth. The Wolverines stood about five feet tall, but were heavily muscled under a thick, shaggy coat of fur. They did resemble a cross between the earth creature of the same name, and an actual wolf, though they walked upright and had opposable thumbs. They were obviously the apex predator of their world, and the Dragon's genetic tampering had given them speech and a human level intelligence. Each Wolverine wore body armor similar to human military, but no helmets. They lived for the hunt, and had no desire to rule, which made them great shock troops for the Dragons. She hoped that they died of heat stroke.

Between them, clad in golden metallic half armor, moved a Dragon. She wondered, sometimes, if the Invy rulers had visited Earth long ago, and created the myth of those legendary creatures. It resembled, more than anything else, one of those long, wispy Chinese serpents, with leathery red skin, but there it stopped. The four true legs walked like a conventional lizard, but there were two more arms that were used to manipulate tools, and vestigial wings. The Invy leader wore gold armor along its torso, which was both ceremonial and incredibly difficult to penetrate with kinetic weapons. It showed their arrogance that they walked through the countryside in highly polished metal that gleamed in the morning sun.

Though the scouts called them by the names of the earth creatures they resembled, they, and their other slave races, were truly alien, and in the tradition of soldiers since the beginning of time, the word "Invaders" had been shortened to "Invy".

"Think they'll get our scent?" asked Singh, who had crawled close to the scout team leader.

"No, probably not," answered Agostine. "The kid," meaning Drummond, "was out with Boyd last night, running our back trail with neutralizer and erasing tracks."

"Thank God for the eggheads in R & D," she said, then fell silent. The patrol was going to come close, but they seemed to be more intent on checking the house than the barn, which is why the team was there, and not in the house.

Then next ten minutes passed in sweltering heat, as they waited for the patrol to pass. The Master Sergeant felt another person crawl up next to him and tug at his sleeve. "Chief," whispered Sergeant Boyd, "we can take them."

"No point. I know you just joined the teams, Mike, but we stay silent and quiet. No fight if we can avoid it."

"They ate your leg, you must hate them even more than I do."

Agostine didn't answer, and the rest of the wait passed in silence, until Drummond gave the all clear. They peeled off their chameleon suits with muttered curses and groans, and sucked down water to replenish the fluids they had lost.

"I would KILL for a shower!" said Griffin.

"As nasty as your cooch is after three weeks in the field, I'm surprised you didn't bring every Wolverine in Upstate New York running!"

"Suck it, Jonesy," she answered.

"No thanks, your booty ain't big enough."

Agostine smiled to himself. Team morale was good. He hummed an old Keith Richards tune under his breath, singing softly about having silver and gold, and returned to his planning. "Regular shifts until nineteen hundred, make sure you sleep, shit and eat. Pre-combat checks and inspections then," said Agostine.

Griffin and Drummond saddled the horses, handing their long guns to other members of the team. Singh passed the submachine gun to Griffin, and the two headed south over the fields.

Chapter 5

Dinner that night at the Warren farm was quiet; the strangers coming by had brought an intrusion into their world. Jeremy sat eating quietly, but seemed restless. Finally, he spoke up.

"Uncle, what did you mean that those travelers weren't farmers? What else is there left to be? Were they traders?" The questions burst out of him, teenage energy running rampant.

His mother spoke first, saying, "Jeremy, the Invy control our world, so you're never going to see more than three people on the road together, but there are some very cruel people out there, even in ones and twos."

"They didn't seem cruel, or bad. Just ... different."

She looked over at her brother, but he looked away, deep in thought. Finally, he spoke. "I think we're going to have to be more careful dealing with the outside world. Yes, the Invy are dangerous, but there are many other dangers."

"Were they bandits?" his nephew asked.

"No, I don't think so." His face was grave and troubled. "They were soldiers. I think they were looking for me."

Victoria's knife dropped on the plate, and the color drained from her face. "David, there ARE no soldiers anymore!"

Jeremy looked back and forth between them, confusion on his face. "I don't understand. The war is over, isn't it? Are we still fighting?"

His uncle slammed his hand down on the table, making the plates jump. "NO!" he exclaimed. "The war is OVER! We LOST!"

"David ..." his sister started to say, alarmed by his outburst. He seemed to grow angrier by the second.

"Victoria, he needs to hear it!"

"Hear what?" asked Jeremy. His uncle was usually a very laid back man; he had rarely seen him even get irritated.

"What I did in the war." He held up his hand when his sister began to object, and she fell silent.

"I was Commander of the Combined Earth Forces." It came out flat, dropping like a bomb on the room.

Jeremy's mouth fell open, and then he laughed. "Yeah, right! You were a private working on computers out in Colorado."

Then he saw the look his mother exchanged, a pleading look that begged him to stop. A growing realization dawned on him when he saw his uncle's answering, hard look.

"Jeremy, it's true."

"But you're like, you were just a teenager then."

David sat back in his chair, and said, "I was part of something called Project Brightstar. The best and the brightest. When that first Invy scout ship took out the International Space Station, it was three years before the actual invasion. Pure accident that they had a reactor failure and we found out about the incoming fleet. If that hadn't happened, we would have been truly fucked."

"DAVID!" said his sister.

"Sorry. Anyway, I was fourteen, and apparently I tested out as the best potential military commander in the United States. There were twelve of us, and I was seventeen when the invaders came. They put me in charge of our defensive fleet, and my friends were our fleet commanders."

"But we lost!" his nephew exclaimed.

"Yes, we did. We lost. I lost." He buried his head in his hands, and Jeremy realized that he was silently sobbing.

"Mom?" he asked, looking at her, astonished to see tears streaming down her own cheeks.

"Jeremy, you don't know what we lost. We lost the world."

A full minute passed in silence, then finally David spoke. "I loved someone, and she was in command of the carrier *Lexington*. The battle was reaching a key point, and maybe I should have ordered her into action, but I couldn't. I knew that it would mean her death. And, well, I could see that we had lost already."

"So what happened?" asked the teen, enthralled.

"We lost, and the Invy got into position to start their orbital bombardment."

"And what happened to the *Lexington*? Was that Kira, the woman you mentioned in your dream?"

His uncle said nothing. "She's dead, isn't she?" asked Jeremy.

"They were holed by a rail gun fighting a rear-guard action. We took a hit on our coms gear and lost the ansible connection at the same time. The whole fleet was lost."

"I'm … sorry, Uncle."

"So yes, all this, the way the world is now, the Invy, six billion or more dead, it's all my fault."

A voice spoke from the corner of the room. "I'm surprised you haven't put a bullet through your head. It would have been the honorable thing to do."

Victoria and Jeremy both jumped, startled, but the former General just answered the voice. "Are you here to do it for me? Make it quick, and let them go."

There was a distortion of light along the wall, and two heavily armed figures were revealed, the strangers from the road. "No, General, we're just here to talk," said the woman.

"Jeremy, Victoria, go upstairs," said David Warren, mind searching for the name of the woman whose face materialized in front of him. The implant provided an answer, long out of date. 2LT Rachel Singh, Virginia Army National Guard, Logistics Branch. The Army photo he saw showed a young, fresh faced woman, barely out of her teens, smiling. The woman in front of him had wisps of gray hair showing, and lines around her eyes that only come from hard combat, though she couldn't be more than her early thirties.

The other person was listed as Master Sergeant Nicholas Agostine, 11Z, skill identifiers B2, B4, F7, J3, P5, S6, S7, W3, W7, W8, 2B, 5W, 6B, E, G, H,V… Operation Enduring Freedom, Spratly War, POW Medal, two Silver Stars, Distinguished Service Cross, …Jesus Christ, the Congressional Medal of Honor…The Special Forces soldier was his nightmare come true, come to kill him.

"But…" his nephew started to object.

"NOW." His uncle's answer was final, and Victoria hustled him up the stairs. Then she came back down and sat at the table. David looked at her, but she returned his gaze until he looked away.

"So, who are you really?" he asked.

"Colonel Rachel Singh, Commander, CEF Scouts Regiment, Ground Forces. This is Master Sergeant Nicholas Agostine."

"And what have you been doing for the past eleven years, Colonel?" he answered, putting heavy sarcasm into her rank. "Wandering the roads like some bandit outlaw? Like the rest of the military after we lost?"

Singh stepped forward, gesturing to a chair. "May I, Ma'am?" she asked of Victoria, then sat before she could give a yes or no. "Sorry, we've been walking a lot."

The other soldier remained standing, his carbine neither pointed directly at them nor away, watching them intently, but with an ear cocked to listen for noises outside.

"So what is it?" asked the former General. "Here to get revenge for our defeat? Go ahead. I think sometimes Victoria wishes it too."

"Why didn't you? Eat a bullet? Hang yourself?" Singh sat with her chin in her fist, staring at him intently.

"Because … I don't know. Mostly because I don't want to give them the satisfaction."

Agostine spoke for the first time, saying "The Invy? You know that they don't know who you are. The last thing Hal did was destroy the internet and all electronic records."

David winced at the name of the Artificial Intelligence that he had spent so much time with. The name 'Hal' had been a bad joke that someone had made when the AI became self-aware, but the computer life form had taken it to heart, and insisted that they use it as his name. They had, in effect, grown up together through the length of Brightstar, Hal becoming sentient the day that David had been inducted. A sudden painful memory surfaced of his friend wishing him good luck and goodbye, before burning out the world's electronic databases, and himself.

His thoughts were interrupted as a large black man, almost a giant, stepped into the room and said, "Reynolds flashed on the laser that there's an Invy patrol moving south on 81, fifteen clicks out. Looks like they're setting up a patrol base for the night. No threat, currently."

Agostine thanked him, and it hit David like a sudden blow. They were real, no shit.

"My God," he said, and felt faint. "You're … you weren't lying. You are who you say you are. There was no Ground Forces, only in contingency planning in case we lost… But, but, what … what have you been doing for eleven years?"

"Watching. Waiting. Gathering intel. Gathering strength. Training. Learning. When the war happened, I was a newly commissioned logistics Lieutenant in the Virginia National Guard. Now, I'm Commander, Scouts Regiment, like I said. There were other things going on, groundside, that you weren't cleared to know about. In case you failed."

She leaned forward, her deep hazel eyes boring into him. "We need your brains, General Warren. You let more than nine billion men, women and children die. You owe your life to them." Then she sat back, interlacing her fingers in front of her, and waited for his answer.

Chapter 6

Outside, Jeremy slid down the beam that supported the porch, something he did on a regular basis without his mother knowing. His feet had barely touched the railing when a powerful arm grabbed his legs and slammed him down onto the porch floor. He struggled until a knee pressed into his back and he felt the metal of a gun barrel touch the side of his head.

"Stop moving, or you're dead," said a deep voice, and Jeremy went completely still. "That's right. I'm not sure your mom would appreciate me blowin your brains all over the place."

"Let him up, Jonesy. Kid ain't going nowhere."

The pressure on his back disappeared, and Jeremy rolled over to see, well, nothing, except the barrel of a gun that seemed to appear out of thin air.

"Sit down, kid. Where were you going?" said an unseen voice from the other side of the porch.

Figuring that he had nothing to lose, and having been raised to be honest, Jeremy answered plainly, "I wanted to listen in on the conversation. Are you guys really soldiers? How come I can't see you?"

"Yes, we're really soldiers. Sergeant First Class Rob Hamilton, Sergeant Isiah Jones, CEF Scout Regiment, Team One. And you can't see us because we're wearing chameleon suits." At that, the man's head appeared. He flashed a quick smile, and then disappeared again.

"So, like, you're fighting the Invy? Can I sign up?"

Jones' voice rumbled in a laugh. "Fight? Now, we don't fight. Are you crazy, boy?"

Jeremy grew indignant at being called boy, and said angrily, "Why the hell don't you?"

"To subdue the enemy without *FIGHTING* is the acme of skill," said Hamilton.

The boy was confused, saying, "Wait, aren't you supposed to fight? Isn't that what soldiers do?"

"Ever seen a Wolverine, boy?" said Jones.

"Of course I have! They came by last week, doing their registry. I've seen them, and a Dragon too."

"Then you know that tangling with them is a quick way to die, and momma Jones' boy ain't in any rush to die."

"So you're cowards, then!" he exclaimed.

"Why don't you ask your uncle what a coward is?"

"That's enough, Jonesy," said Hamilton, but without any real passion in his voice.

There was silence for a moment, and then Jones appeared, and held up a set of binoculars to his face. "Message coming in from Reynolds, Invy 15 clicks I-81 condition yellow."

"Go tell the Colonel," said Hamilton.

"What does condition yellow mean? Are you going to fight them?" asked Jeremy.

"Kid, get it through your thick head. We lost. There isn't any fighting anymore. Maybe someday, but not right now."

Jones reappeared, and then disappeared again. "Colonel's waiting on his answer. I don't think he's going to come along."

"That's his choice," answered the disembodied voice of Hamilton. "Get yourself back upstairs before your mother finds you out, kid."

"Just tell me one thing, first. How do I join you guys?" The pleading in the teen's voice was obvious.

"Well, first you have to kill a Wolverine in battle, barehanded," answered the deep disembodied voice.

"JONES! That IS enough," said the higher-ranking NCO. "You can't join us, kid. Not for a long while yet. The CEF is pretty damn selective. Now git."

With a dramatic sigh, Jeremy climbed back up onto the roof and then slid into his bedroom through the open window. Then he leaned up against his slightly open door, trying to hear further conversation, perking up when he heard the screen door slam again.

"He's not going," said the voice of a woman, the one with the strange accent.

"Damned coward," said Jonesy, and Jeremy burned with shame. He felt the anger rise within him, and his face flushed red, fighting back tears.

Downstairs, his mother started arguing with his uncle, muted words that he couldn't make out. Turning up his oil lamp, he got up and started rummaging through his closet, stuffing dark clothes into his knapsack.

He waited until the windup clock next to his bed said midnight, and slipped down the stairs. Jeremy crept past his uncle, who was sitting at his desk, lamp turned low, with his head buried in his hands, and moved slowly into the mudroom. Muscles tense with the effort to move silently, he lifted the AK-74 up off the pegs on the wall, stuffed two magazines into his pockets, and moved ever so slowly, opening the screen door. Gently closing it, he headed towards his only friend's place, three miles down the road.

Chapter 7

People who lived outside the Invy permitted towns did so in small households of no more than three. Regular patrols came and searched homesteads, and when there were more than three, the youngest person found was slaughtered for food. It might be two or even three years between searches, but eventually they would come. Jeremy hadn't seen it happen, but his uncle and mother had, and his friend Tommy Gates had had his little sister fed to the Wolverines. It was, his uncle had said, a way to keep the population under control.

"It's better," he had said, "than what happened between 30 degrees north and south. They wiped out every single human being with some kind of virus." They had gotten that news a few years ago, from a refugee moving north.

Jeremy knew that Tommy would be on-board with his plan. His friend hated them, and had often talked about fighting, though neither teen had clue one about how to go about it. If there actually WAS a resistance, then maybe the CEF would take them both if they had done some damage.

He jogged the three miles in little more than half an hour, used to walking everywhere, and tapped on Tommy's ground floor window. It took a minute of whispered conversation, but in the end, his friend joined him with his .22 rifle and a dozen rounds of ammo.

"Do you think that will be enough?" asked Jeremy.

His friend, who was a year younger and bulky from hard work on his family's small farm, answered with confidence. "I can kill a squirrel three hundred yards away. If we get close enough, I'll put one through a Wolverine's eye. That'll take 'em down."

They moved silently across the dark land, knowing it intimately, cutting across the hills that ran north south, using dusty, cracked, two lane side roads. The countryside around was empty except for small farms every couple of miles, centered on older houses that had been able to fall back on nineteenth century tech.

"How do you know there'll be a patrol there?" asked Tommy.

"I saw one heading down Route 20 today, just before dark. You know they'll probably cut up 81 to get to Syracuse, and maybe they'll stop for the night." He felt bad lying to his friend, but he wanted to keep the knowledge of the scouts to himself until they had something to show for it.

They crested the last rise, and, sure enough, there were lights showing around two vehicles parked among the rusted-out wrecks on the highway. Both of them were experts in the woods, and they slowly made their way down to where an on-ramp formed a berm that shielded them from view, moving from cover to cover.

"How are we going to do this?" asked Tommy, who was beginning to have doubts about what they were doing, once the excitement had worn off a bit. Things had been quiet for years, and neither really had any experience with the aliens, other than occasional trips to an Invy controlled town and the occasional registration patrols. The memory of his baby sister had faded over time, and though his hatred burned, it was getting doused with cold reality.

"I'll move over about a hundred yards and empty the AK at the vehicles," answered Jeremy. "Then while they're looking for me, you shoot one of them. We can use the berm for cover and get back over the hill. They'll never know what hit them."

"Got it!" said Tommy enthusiastically, now that there was an actual plan.

Jeremy disappeared into the darkness with a whispered, "Wait for it!"

"Ziv, we got movement," whispered Reynolds. In her rifle scope, she watched as the heat signature of two individuals crept within a hundred meters of the Invy patrol base, using the berm for cover. She wished like hell she could use the laser range finder on her optics, but the Invy would flip their shit just from the backscatter. Their sensors were great, on a tactical level, supported by their armor.

The Serb crawled over and turned on his own spotting scope, bigger than the rifles, with a greater field of view. The passive IR system quickly showed the two human figures, the active range card overlay he had programed in earlier giving a rough approximation of their distance.

"Can you identify?" They had been on overwatch for the last three days, cataloguing the people who had come and gone up the main highway. The Invy patrol had passed south earlier that night, around dusk, and the information had been sent by com light to the rest of the team while they were at Warren's house. It was bounced off a light scatterer mounted on an old cell phone tower, and Jones had picked up the weak light on his NVGs. The Invy sensors were good on their vehicles, but oriented to detect threats aimed at them.

"No," she answered, "but they look smaller than an adult. Kids maybe?"

Zivcovic dialed up the magnification to confirm, though it didn't have the resolution of the rifle scope. He watched as they separated, and one moved to their left, using abandoned cars to hide his movements from the Invy.

"Be ready to engage," he said. "It looks like those idiots are planning to start some trouble. There are six wolverines and one Dragon, correct?"

"Correct, though the Dragon is buttoned up in the front vehicle," she answered. "You know our orders. No interference with any locals."

"Fuck our orders. If someone is going to kill wolverines, I am going to help them. We can snipe from here, use them as a distraction. Who knows, maybe they'll actually do some damage, and we can bag a few."

"They'll have dazzlers on the vehicles."

He snorted dismissively, and said, "We're over fifteen hundred meters away, and uphill. It will not matter to us."

She knew how much he hated them, and felt the same. The redhead grimly settled down in her perch as her sergeant switched over to his own rifle. Normally they acted as shooter / spotter, but if things went to shit, then it was targets of opportunity. She settled the crosshairs on the Wolverine wearing the silver badge of *Hashut*, or Senior Sergeant, as it slept curled up near a track, and she waited, slowly inhaling and exhaling, trying to keep her heart rate slow.

His heart racing wildly, Jeremy crouched behind a wrecked station wagon, and checked the chamber of the rifle for the hundredth time. He had hunted plenty of animals, and tried hard to think of the Invy that way. As he sat and tried to find courage, he thought about the world that had been denied him, and a fierce anger rose up.

The rifle felt good and solid in his hands, and he flicked the selector lever up one click, to AUTO. Another notch up would have made it single shot, and more accurate, but he wanted to strike hard, get their attention, and get away, leaving a shot to Tommy. Slowly rising and laying the barrel across the ruined hood, the teenager sighted on the camp, almost two hundred yards away, and pulled the trigger. All eleven rounds fired off, the barrel climbing skyward and then thumping down, back onto the hood. Jeremy screamed in exaltation, and yelled, "That's for Earth, you bastards!"

Reynolds fired as soon as she saw the flicker of the discharges washing over the target, before the burst even finished. In her IR scope, when her Barret 50 settled down, she saw that the big bullet had left a bright glow splattered on the ground, and the Wolverine NCO had disappeared.

She was up and moving, not risking a second shot, but Zivcovic was even faster, grabbing his ruck and heading towards the two horses that were tethered downhill and behind them. Insanely bright lights erupted behind them, bathing the valley in brilliance, and they heard the hiss crack of plasma weapons discharging.

Chapter 8

"I want to go back and do some Battle Damage Assessment," said Zivcovic. The Serb always liked to see what he hit, and it drove his partner crazy.

Reynolds shook her head in disagreement, saying, "You know those two are deader than shit, and we need to get back to the barn and report to the Team. Aren't you worried about the Invy swarming this place?"

"Cache the weapons, we will go see what the effects are before it is light. You know what will happen, what they will do, within a day."

She did know. When the dazzlers went off, 360 degree holo was taken, capturing the faces and features of everyone caught in it. The Invy registration archives used facial recognition software to identify the people behind the attack, and was usually successful against irregulars. It was their standard response, the kinetic equivalent of dropping a two thousand pound bomb on the family of anyone responsible. It was why the CEF forces operated so quietly, avoiding conflict, and why it was so hard to get people to cooperate. Last year, outside Boston, she had been on an intelligence gathering operation that had gone bad, trying to steal some tech; the Invy had actually pulled out of one of the safe towns and turned it into a giant crater. Five thousand people, gone in an instant, after a shootout. She and Zivcovic had only survived because they had been outside, providing overwatch, as they had been tonight.

"OK, but not too close. You're a little brash, Sasha," she said, concern and caring leaking into her voice.

He grinned a skull like grin, and said, "I do not know this English word, brash, but I like it. Sounds tough, like me."

Jeremy had run as fast as he could, blinded by the Invy lights, tripping over debris in the road, and finally falling and rolling down the side of the highway. As he did, a plasma bolt took off his leg just below the knee, and real darkness overcame him. The last thing he had seen, before the Dazzler had struck him, was Tommy, standing to fire, and his friend's head vanishing in a puff of red tinged steam.

Now he lay face up in a ditch on the side of the road, run off from a stream washing over him, and cried bitter tears, sobbing incoherently. He had fallen through some dense overgrowth, to land with a muted splash, and the cool water had woken him slightly. Jeremy pulled himself downstream to where a drain pipe crossed under the road, and used the last of his strength to slide inside. His leg felt numb and burning at the same time, confused signals from the cauterized limb rocketing through his brain, and like a wild, wounded animal, he sought some deep hole to die in.

Others had found shelter there before, and twenty feet into the darkness, his blind hands encountered bones, and what he finally made out be a skull. He gave up then, and passed out.

As Zivcovic and Reynolds watched from their hidden perch a few hundred meters away, more than an hour after the attack, two wolverines, accompanied by a gold armored Dragon, slowly made their way up the road, one sniffing at the ground. The furred creature suddenly yipped and turned off the road, towards them. The other trooper dropped to all fours, slinging his plasma rifle across his back, and followed. The Dragon stayed on the road, but hissed orders at them. They barked back, and started to follow the ditch downstream.

"They're telling the Dragon they have a scent trail. Looks like one got away," said Reynolds. Zivcovic had never bothered to try to understand the yips, barks and growls that were the wolverine language, but Reynolds had made a passionate study out of it.

"Well, he's dead now," answered the non-com.

"Probably," she whispered back. They were peering out from under IR neutral blankets, downwind of the enemy. The Invy troops had reached what looked like a culvert that cut back under the road, and engaged in a bit of an argument. Then they started back towards the Dragon.

Zivcovic raised his carbine; the sniper rifles were broken down and stashed with the horses, five hundred meters over the next rise. "We can take them," he muttered, almost as much to himself as to her.

"We can't," she whispered. "Right now, they can write it off to a bunch of stupid kids, or bandits, especially with that body on the road. A secondary ambush is going to bring a world of shit down on this whole area." God, he was a bloodthirsty bastard. His rifle tracked across them for a few seconds more, then lowered.

"They said something about old death and new death," said Reynolds. "Looks as if our friend made it into the culvert and died. They like their meat live, and fresh. By the time they dig his carcass out, it will be a couple hours old, not worth it." The three Invy made their way back down the highway, entered one of the vehicles, and drove north toward Syracuse, leaving the other APC sitting idly, fusion plant turning over.

A furious argument erupted between the sniper and her boss. Zivcovic wanted to search the battle site for possible dropped Invy tech, including weapons; Reynolds cautioned him that the AI aboard the idling APC would, in her words, smoke the shit out of them when they got within a hundred meters. That and the patrol would return in an hour with a new crew for the abandoned track. He ignored her protestations and slid out from under the blanket, quickly moving in a crouch through the same stream bed the wolverines had explored earlier.

Reynolds cursed and hustled after him; scouts never deserted their partners. They had just reached the drain pipe, and were about to climb up onto the road itself, when a low groan echoed out of the pipe.

"Wait!" exclaimed Reynolds, and she bent down to listen at the opening. She heard it again, a pain-filled, quiet sound. If they had been any later, the birds singing at dawn would have hidden it. She put her carbine down and crawled into the tunnel, further and further, until her now lit headlamp showed a single boot, surrounded by bones.

"Ziv!" she called back down the tunnel. "He's alive!"

"Kill him, quickly!" answered the Serb.

If he could ignore orders, so could she. The tough woman grabbed hold of the leg and started pulling; it was hard to move the dead weight, and she was sweating in the July humidity by the time she exited the tunnel.

Zivcovic rolled the man over, to reveal a boyish face. "I know him, it is Warren's nephew," he said flatly, and pulled out his knife. It was over a foot long, and razor sharp.

"Let's bring him back; Doc can take a look at him. His leg has been cauterized, he might make it."

Zivcovic thought about it for a full minute, blade laying against the teen's throat, watching his carotid artery jump under the knife. The teen was pale, probably in shock, and his pulse seemed erratic. "He is going to die anyway," said the Serb, and then rolled the boy sideways. The knife slashed deeply, and blood ran black in the pre-dawn light.

She knew he was right; carrying a wounded person cross country with Invy patrols out would get them both killed, and the boy was dying anyway. There was no way to treat him in the field, and if they had brought him to an Invy town, to a clinic, the plasma burn would be a dead giveaway. Still, she remembered a world, not so long ago, where he would be in a hospital and living. Hell, in that other world, his worst injury would have come from playing football.

"You stupid, brave kid," she said harshly, and squeezed her own eyes tight, fighting back tears.

Zivcovic stood up and said, "Come, help me hide the body. Then we must go back to the Team."

"SCOUTS COMING IN!" called Boyd, who was on watch at the north side of the barn. The door rolled open, and the two snipers almost jumped from their horses. They had ridden hard cross country, and the animals' sides were heaving.

Zivcovic snapped a quick salute at Colonel Singh, but made his report to Master Sergeant Agostine. "Warren's nephew and someone else attacked an Invy patrol about two hours ago on I-81. They're both dead, but they probably got an ID off facial recognition after they were hit by dazzlers."

"Shit!" exclaimed the veteran NCO, and the team sprang to life around him. "Boyd, Jones, you're with me and the Colonel. Doc, you're going to switch off with me when we get Warren, you go with the Colonel and I'll take him. Snipers on overwatch, you all know the rally point and the exfil plan, but we have to move, NOW!"

"What about the sister?"

"She comes along or not. We don't care about her."

Their biggest issue was time. How long would it take the Invy to ID the attackers? He looked to his own gear and weapons as the sniper team galloped off, to get to the rally point and set up.

Chapter 9

They didn't bother with the chameleon suits. The sun was just rising and the five scouts ran across the fields. The suits were made for stealth and hiding, and were incredibly hot. Speed was of the essence, and they moved from cover to cover, trying to avoid the Invy drones that were sure to be out now.

Reaching the rear door, Hamilton stepped back, removed a sledge hammer from his pack, and swung hard. The lock shattered, and Jones went past him, followed by Boyd. They moved into the kitchen, weapons up, and called, "CLEAR!"

"GENERAL WARREN!" yelled Agostine. "WARREN!" he yelled again, and the man appeared at the head of the stairs, looking sleepy and half awake.

"What the hell?" he muttered, still trying to take in the sight of armed men at the bottom of the stairs. His sister appeared behind him, a pistol clutched in her hand. Jones raised his rifle, but Agostine pushed it downward.

"Please come down," he said to them. "We have some news you need to listen to."

"OK," said Warren, and the two came quietly downstairs. At the bottom he stopped, but Victoria started to go back upstairs.

"Ma'am," said Colonel Singh in her soft voice, "please come into the living room."

"I have to go wake Jeremy up. He deserves to hear whatever you have to say." Then she caught the look that passed between Singh and Agostine, and her face went pale.

"J, Boyd, go pull security. Get signal with Ziv and let us know if anything is approaching."

The two men went out the front door this time, pulling out their chameleon suits and disappearing before they even got into the hallway. The rest moved into the living room, but remained standing.

Singh spoke first, directly to Victoria. "Mrs. Stalh, early this morning your son, along with someone else, attacked an Invy patrol.

It was observed by our sniper team, and both were killed in the action."

Doc had been expecting her to faint, but she didn't, though her knees buckled. Then she turned, and slapped her brother across the face, a ringing smack that reeled him backwards. Faster than any of them could move, she pulled her pistol from the waistband of her sweats and pointed it at his face.

"GET OUT!" she screamed, her voice shrill.

"Victoria…" he started to protest. She ignored the guns that were pointed at her, and moved closer, holding the .45 inches from his face, hammer cocked back.

"He's dead because of you! All your stories, he looked up to you, and had to prove himself. MY SON! GET THE HELL OUT OF MY HOUSE!" she screeched again, pushed the barrel into his face.

Warren cringed backwards, and slowly moved towards the hall. Agostine and Hamilton moved out in front of him, and Singh stepped towards her.

"Mrs. Stahl, the Invy will destroy this place at any moment. Come with us," she said as calmly as she could, feeling the woman's pain.

The pistol swung to point at her, and Victoria hissed, "Get the hell out of my house!"

Singh turned and walked slowly out the door, following the two NCOs. Outside on the porch, the men held David Warren as he struggled to go back into the house.

"Let. Me. GO!" he said angrily, grief tearing at his voice.

Singh stood in front of him, and said, "General, we need to leave. A thunderbolt may strike this place at any minute, and there will be increased Invy patrols."

"My sister needs me!" he raged, and struggled even more. "VAL!" he yelled.

Inside, she heard him yelling; saw nothing but the last photograph she had of her son, when he was four, just before the invasion. He was dressed in a baseball uniform that said "SLUGGER" on it, with a broad smile on his face, and the grass was green around him,. Her husband, dead eleven years now, had him on his shoulders, and their happy faces looked out at the camera.

She took the picture down off the mantle, sat on the couch, and placed it in her lap. Ignoring the continued shouts from outside, she whispered one more time to her family.

The shot was muffled, even though the windows were open to let in the breeze, making everyone freeze when it rang out.

"VAL!" screamed Warren, and broke one arm free from Boyd, though Jones held him in an iron grip.

"Doc, go check it out. Jonesy, quiet him down!" ordered Agostine. The medic went back into the house, as Jones wrapped an invisible arm around Warren's neck and slowly squeezed. The man struggled for a bit, then fell silent. Boyd left them there, stepped out from under the overhanging porch, and activated his suit, watching down the road.

Hamilton came back out, wiping bloody hands on a towel. "She didn't do it right, I had to put her down." The medic didn't say anything more, but the image of the woman, half her face blown away and an eyeball popped out, rolling in agony on the floor, would never leave him. None of the dead ever did.

"Nick," said the disembodied voice of Sergeant Boyd out in the yard, "according to the schedule, the next orbital should be in range in less than five minutes. If there's not a strike then, we have a half an hour."

"OK, folks, let's head to the RP. J, you carry the General until he's able to walk."

The black man appeared, folding his cham suit and stuffing it onto the carrier at his side, and slung the groggy, smaller man over his shoulder. "Just cause I'm so big, I always get stuck doing the heavy shit!" he muttered, but set off in a loping run, around the back of the house and southwest. Boyd appeared next to him, and the two moved off.

"Should we burn it?" asked Singh.

"No, it won't be here after today. Probably not till later, but still, it will be gone. Let's go," answered Agostine, and the three set off in the scout walk/jog that ate up the miles, following in Jones' and Boyd's footsteps.

They made it over the rise and changed course due west to climb the ridge that led to the rally point. Before they had gone more than half a mile, a light appeared high in the east, first a pinprick, then rushing towards them with increasing speed.

"EVERYONE DOWN!" yelled Boyd, who had seen it first. The entire team hit the ground, lying flat and clutching the earth, clapping hands over their ears and opening their mouths. Warren, having regained consciousness, lay there unaware of - or simply not caring about - what was happening.

The tungsten rod, about five feet long and six inches wide, hit slightly to the east of the house at over seven thousand miles per hour. The force of the impact vaporized the ground where it hit with the equivalent of five tons of high explosive, digging far into the ground and vaporizing the bedrock.

There didn't seem to be any sound, just the feeling of your lungs wanting to be ripped out of your chest from the blast. The ground heaved under them, throwing everyone up a few inches, and the shockwave rolled over them a split second later, hammering them back into the ground. The air rushed past, away from them at first, then rushing back, followed by pieces of earth, stone and wood pelting down around them.

Boyd yelled as a large piece of cinderblock landed on the back of his knee, smashing it. The rest were lucky, only receiving small bruises. After a minute, Warren stood, and saw a small mushroom cloud rising where his home had been.

"Mother of God," he said, and sat back down. His ears were ringing from the explosion.

Hamilton, looking to Boyd's knee, said, with clear disdain, "I guess you're all in now, General Coward."

Chapter 10

They made it to the rally point on top of the ridge, picked up Zivcovic and Reynolds, and set up perimeter security while Doc assessed Boyd's leg and they planned their next move. Warren sat by himself in the center of the perimeter, while Singh and Agostine talked. Three miles away, another cloud carried off the remains of Tommy's parents.

"I hope he's worth it. We were seriously exposed on this op," said Agostine, using the time to clean his weapons. Singh didn't answer for a minute, looking at Warren. He seemed a pathetic wreck, and started crying even as she met his eyes.

Turning back to Agostine, she said, "Nick, the time is coming. The kids outside the towns are growing up uneducated, and the ones in the towns are getting brainwashed. All of us veterans are getting older. Pretty soon we're not going to be able to fight this fight and hope to win."

"Can we win?" he asked, sharpening his knife. Every few seconds he looked around to check the team's dispositions.

"Maybe. It all depends on disposition of forces, timing, and planning. What we need him for, more than anything else, is to sharp shoot the plan. There's nobody else left with his training and experience."

"Well, he's going to shit himself when he meets Archangel."

"You're not supposed use code word IDs in the field," she reprimanded him.

"When the hell ARE we supposed to use them, Kali?" he answered with a grin.

Her dusky face took on a frown. "I'm a Sikh, we're monotheistic. I can't believe they gave me that."

"I dunno, I think it fits! Destruction and all…" The officer threw a rock at him, and he laughed.

"Careful," she said, while still smiling, "I could have you shot."

Agostine grinned and said, "I've been shot before, and I've seen you shoot, I'm not wor-."

An excited shout interrupted them, Jonesy calling, "WOLVERINES! No Dragons!"

"Shit!" cursed the NCO. "Investigating the thunderbolt effects. Must have picked up our scent. What do you want to do, Colonel?"

"I will take the horses and General Warren to Raven Rock. I assume your team can handle themselves?"

He knew that she wasn't leaving because of cowardice. Rachel Singh had been among the first scouts, and some of her infiltrations were legendary. It was just that she was an outsider in a unit that was extremely close and worked well together.

"Got it. Doc, help Warren onto his horse. Get the long guns out, we're going to need them. Boyd stand fast, Jones on me, we're going to swing left and hit them from the side. This is going to draw a shitstorm down on us. Doc, Ziv and Reynol… Jesus effing Christ, not again!"

Zivcovic had dropped all his equipment and body armor, quickly taking off his shirt to reveal a heavily tattooed body covered with slashing scars. He pulled his foot-long fighting knife from its sheath, and set off in a run past the startled Boyd.

"Jonesy, stop that asshole!" said Reynolds.

The black man just held up his hands in a "who, me?" gesture, knowing full well the Serb was as likely to gut him as the enemy. Zivcovic flashed a grin as he ran past Jones, who shook his head.

"What is he doing?" asked the bewildered Warren.

"That dumbass is going to challenge the Wolverine Squad Leader to single combat," answered Reynolds.

"That's insane!" he said, trying to control his horse, which was jittery from the excitement.

"Yup!" she answered, nodded to Colonel Singh, and smacked the horse on the ass. It took off at a quick trot, and Singh followed on hers.

"OK, let's go watch," said Hamilton. "Even if he doesn't get killed, the stupid ass is going to get torn to shit again."

The entire team, except for Hamilton, activated their chameleon suits and moved out, down the path the Serb had taken. When they hit the tree line, they spread out into concealed positions to watch. Hamilton stepped out into full view; it would be assumed by the Invy that the man advancing across the field to them would be traveling with a companion. No one walked alone.

The Wolverines had seen Zivcovic, and one stepped forward. He wore the silver badge of a *Hashut*, and was probably the patrol leader. There was gray on his muzzle, and though he only stood a little under five feet on his hind legs, powerful muscles rippled under his skin, and the ripping claw on each hand/paw was sheathed in shining steel. Vicious canine teeth attested to the creature's predatory nature, before they had been uplifted, and their plasma rifles curved around their thumb and three true fingers. His squad growled and barked and yipped, until he turned and struck one in the nose with his rifle. They fell silent, backing down low to the ground.

"Damn, they're kinda ugly and beautiful at the same time, ain't they?" whispered Boyd, who had lain down next to his team chief. Agostine started to reprimand him for not staying put with his bad leg, but then stopped.

"They're killing machines, I'll give them that," answered Agostine, and unconsciously tapped his prosthetic.

"Did they do that to you?" Boyd asked.

Agostine nodded a yes, and whispered back, "In the fighting pits. I forgot, you're Main Force, haven't really been exposed to the Invy in combat."

The new scout raised his rifle scope and looked at the Wolverine Non-Com, who seemed to be doing some elaborate challenge ritual, yipping and barking at Ziv. The human stood calmly, blade held low and ready, and chanted back at it in Serbian.

"I've heard about this, the challenge," said Boyd. "If he kills the patrol leader, we go free? What if they kill Ziv?"

It was a moment before he got a reply. "Then we run for our goddamned lives, and give Colonel Singh enough time to get away with Warren."

"Does he have a shot?"

Again, another pause, then, "The odds are going to catch up with him eventually. This is the fourth time he's done this, no one else has survived more than one."

Silence from both the patrol and the scouts as the Wolverine completed his ritual, grounded his body armor and weapons, and turned to face Zivcovic.

"Watch and learn, Mike. We think the Wolverines know about the existence of our forces, the Scout Teams at least, but they don't tell the Dragons. I'm pretty sure they think it will ruin their sport. If there was a Dragon with them, we'd be in deep shit right now."

With a cry of "URAAAAH!" the Serb launched himself forward, and the Wolverine answered with a wolf-like howl, both arms extended to slash inward.

Chapter 11

Although he pissed her off constantly, Zivcovic was Reynolds' partner, and sometimes more in the dark of night. Her heart beat wildly in fear as the two met; there was a flash of steel in the summer sunlight, and then they sprang apart. Several bloody streaks exposed themselves on Ziv's back, where the ripping claws had scored him, but the Wolverine was limping badly from a deep stab wound on his leg.

The creature held up both arms, and crossed the bloody steel claws in salute. The Serb raised his own reddened knife in return, and they started to circle each other. Reynolds could see that one cut had actually laid the skin open to his ribs, and muscles could be seen moving under the bloody tear.

With a howl, the alien charged forward again, low, trying for Ziv's hamstrings. His claw pierced the bottom of the leg, and Ziv stumbled sideways to prevent the muscle and tendons from being ripped out. As he did, he pivoted, and drove the chisel point of his knife down hard on the Wolverine's shoulder blade, burying it several inches deep through the tough pelt, then withdrawing it, rolling away from a backslash.

Again they separated, but this time, there was no ceremonial salute. Both knew that they were in the fight of their lives. One alien trooper raised his plasma rifle, but another wearing the bronze disk of an *Afshut*, or Corporal, knocked it downward with a harsh bark.

Warily, both bleeding heavily and sides heaving with breath, they stood two meters apart, each waiting on the other to make a move. Then the *Hashut*, shaking his head, seemingly to clear it, drool flying from his jaws, launched himself in another low stab, intending to gut the human with an upward stroke. Ziv rolled to the side at the last minute, and the razor-sharp blade flicked out, seeming to disappear into the fur at the side of the creature's neck. In return, a ripping claw caught the side of his face, tearing more than slicing from eye to ear, and the Wolverine's teeth sank deeply into his arm, leaving a ragged slash.

Each regained their footing, and turned to face their foe again. The Wolverine could barely stand, and blood flowed freely from his neck, shoulder and leg. Gathering strength, the thing rose up to its full height, let out a weak, trembling howl, and then fell forward, dead.

Pandemonium erupted from the five remaining Wolverines, barks and howls, but they held their place. The triumphant human walked over to the prostrate form and cut the two ripping claws off. Then, staggering, he moved to the *Afshut*, and handed him the long fighting knife. The Corporal took it and sheathed it in his belt, then barked an order. Two of them moved out and collected the *Hashut's* body, placing it in the back of their APC, and the rest filed in. With a rising whine, it spun up on its air cushion and headed north, following the dirt road.

Hamilton ran forward, grabbing at his aide bag. When he got to the Serb, he saw that the damage was worse than he feared. One eye might be a loss, sliced directly across, and the deep cut along his back was raw and leaking blood profusely, mirroring the wound on his leg.

"You stupid fuck, you're going to die from infection," he muttered as he started to field dress the wounds and injected nanos.

"Doc, I am champion still, yes?" answered Zivcovic weakly, with a bloody grin.

"You're going to lose that eye, dickhead, and maybe the arm too," Hamilton answered, "but yeah, you're a damned legend now."

"Good! Maybe Singh go on date with me now?" said the bloody form, and he passed out.

Hamilton grunted, tying off another bandage and starting an IV, saying to the unconscious form, "The stupid shit we do to impress women, I swear." He heard someone approaching, and didn't look up, in case there were more patrols and sensors, not wanting to give away someone in a chameleon suit.

"Is he going to make it?" asked Master Sergeant Agostine.

"I'm going to need blood from Jones and Boyd, and he's going to lose that eye and possibly the arm, but yeah, he'll make it. He's too stupid and stubborn to die."

He heard Agostine breathe out, then say, "We can meet you at hide Viking, there's power there and some medical supplies. It's about forty miles, though, so you can take the two other horses."

"OK, if we push, I can get him there in a day. I hope it's not too much on him."

"Give us three days to meet you. Do your best, he just saved our lives."

Hamilton knew that, but he still hated patching people up for what he considered stupidity. "Yeah, and he's going to be insufferable when he wakes up."

The medic left him lying on the ground, and went back to the tree line, where Reynolds had brought up the two remaining horses.

"Can I go with you?" she asked, knowing better, but unable to keep the concern out of her voice.

"Nope. No more than three on the road, you know that, and they're going to check us out if there are three of us, and one wounded."

She nodded, and removed her Barrett .50 and Zivcovic's M-2010; both would be cached in hidden air tight canisters at the nearest weapons hide point, about ten miles away in a ruined town. The others' carbines would join the sniper rifles.

"Alright, people, let's move out," said Agostine. "Jones, you team with Boyd. Reynolds, you're with me."

Jonesy rumbled from his hidden position, "Boyd, I'm going to have to snuggle with you for body heat. If you catch my drift."

"Really?" asked the new scout, a tone of doubt in his voice.

"Knock it off, J," countered Agostine. "Boyd, he's kidding."

"I'm not!" Boyd answered, "I'm a former sailor!"

They departed at ten minute intervals, after Doc had transfused blood into Zivcovic. "He's lucky he didn't get a major vein or artery cut, idiot," he told Reynolds as she helped him stitch the wounds closed.

"Doc," mumbled the Zivcovic, "give me pain killers. I am done being tough guy for now."

"No, you're not. Suck it up, buttercup. We've got miles to cover before dark." Jones helped him get Zivcovic slung over the saddle, and they rode away south along the ridge.

Boyd and Jonesy were next to leave, heading west towards I-81. Reynolds and Agostine would parallel them, going down Route 13. Before they went, the younger soldier asked about pursuit.

"The Invy will give them twenty-four hours to clear the area, and therefore us," answered Jonesy, whose ghetto accent seemed to disappear when things got serious. "Like the man told you, Boyd, the Wolverines suspect the existence of organized resistance, but they have a weird code of honor, and they've been beat. Leader of the pack bullshit, I guess, but good enough for us." He shouldered his light machine gun and said, "See you at Viking in two, three days. It'll be good to take a shower."

They disappeared into the woods, and Agostine turned to Reynolds. "Ziv's going to make it," he told her.

"I hope so," she answered, "because I'm going to kill him!" Her boss laughed, and they started walking southwest at a brisk pace.

Chapter 12

Major Takara Ikeda, CEF Scout Regiment (Far East), formerly of JDF Special Forces, lay perfectly still in the forest surrounding the Invy air base on Honshu, outside the ruins of Tokyo. He relaxed his breathing, calming his heartbeat, touching his inner *wa*.

The chameleon suit held his body heat in, converting it into electricity and directing it downward through a static line that was pegged deep into the ground. The heavy July heat also helped mask his IR signature, and he ignored the sweat running down his face.

Fifty meters away on a runway, a squat Invy shuttlecraft sat, engines throbbing with power, antigrav spooling up. The pilot, a *tako*, or octopus, hung by two limbs in the doorway, running system checks with some of his other arms and a tablet.

Ikeda ran through his own checklist, reviewing the flight controls from the simulator at CEF Far East Headquarters. Over five hundred flight hours, but it was all theory. No one had ever actually captured a functioning Invy craft. The majority of controls were through the pilot's helmet mounted sensors, and designed for eight tentacles and two true hands, but they thought they had a work around patch using the emergency controls.

He put the thoughts aside and dialed up the gain on his night vision goggles, scanning slowly left and right. THERE! he thought. A wheeled transport was approaching; riding in the open cab was a Dragon and two Wolverines. They pulled up to a stop at the ramp into the transport, and all three disembarked. The two guards took up station at either side of the ramp, while the gold armored Dragon made his way in. His Scout Team had been watching this airfield for five months, and there seemed to be a regularly scheduled flight, according to some strange calendar the Invy used. Ikeda had been waiting here for three days.

He thanked the Americans and their R & D department that had come up with the scent neutralizer. The Wolverines sight wasn't all that great, but they could smell you from a mile away, and he didn't want to tangle with them on the ground. It would completely blow the plan, and probably end his life.

The guards moved up the ramp; it whispered shut, and the engines rose to a sharp whine. Ikeda toggled the mini oxygen bottle that fed into his face mask, counted *San, Ni, Ichi*, and took off running. He cleared the fifty meters as if a Wolverine were chasing him, grabbed onto the side access ladder, and vaulted upwards, swinging himself up onto the roof of the shuttle as it lifted into the air, quickly centering himself to prevent the pilot from sensing an imbalance. Then he waited as the craft rose upward, swung about, and headed southwest, out over the Sea of Japan.

After five minutes, they had reached a cruising altitude of thirty thousand feet, almost ten kilometers up, moving at a leisurely 200 kph. He rapidly grew colder, and gratefully sucked at the oxygen, then felt the craft lurch as it hit some turbulence, almost causing him to lose grip of the small magnetic grapnels that held him in place.

His mind reviewed the time table, and right at the exact second he expected, his watch buzzed in alarm. Behind him, most of the way down the craft, sat the secondary power plant access hatch, used for maintenance and moving large parts in and out. Moving very carefully, lying on his stomach, the wind tearing at him, he made his way to the hatch, then activated the Invy laser cutting torch that was strapped to his arm, aiming at the hatch seal.

With a BANG, the hatch flipped up, caught the airstream, and slammed backwards, making the ship buck wildly. Depressurized, the air howled out of the opening, and he waited until it had equalized. As the pilot fought for control, taking it into a steep dive to get to better air pressure, Ikeda swung himself down and out of the slipstream, into the cramped engine compartment, and unstrapped the heavy bag he had slung around his shoulders. As he had practiced a thousand times, he found the main communications relay, and placed a capacitor against it, then set a timer for sixty seconds. When it discharged, the shuttle's communications and tracking beacon went with it. Taking off the restricting suit hood as the dive leveled out, he crouched back and waited for the engine access doorway to open, *wakizashi* held ready, as they fell to a breathable altitude.

The first Wolverine opened the door, and Ikeda stabbed straight into the creature's side, seeking the joint in its body armor, feeling the blade drive deep. Then he let go and struck with a Karate *Tate Empi Uchi*, feeling his elbow crunch into the thing's soft muzzle, stunning it long enough for the double heart to stop beating.

Reaching down and pulling out the short sword, he stepped into the corridor that led to the cockpit, moving as silently as possible. He heard the pilot chittering on their coms, probably declaring an in-flight emergency, which was by the plan.

The taser in his hand centered on the back of the Dragon, who had an oxygen mask over its lizard face. The other Wolverine sat strapped into its seat, nervously pawing its fur and barking at the pilot. Then something must have betrayed the Japanese officer's presence; the body guard unlatched and spun, throwing itself at him, lightning fast. Ikeda swung his arm holding the taser and pulled the trigger, and the darts, extra heavy to pierce Dragon hide or Wolverine fur, smashed into the pilot, sending thousands of volts into the eight-limbed creature.

The craft immediately rolled, throwing the scout and the wolverine to the floor, and he felt the sharp ripper claw bury into his left arm, then wrench back out; the pain was immediate and intense. Then the autopilot kicked in and they rolled level. With his good hand, Ikeda struck at the nerve junction on the side of the Wolverine's neck, stunning it, and barely missing another swing of the claw. Through this, the Dragon watched impassively, strapped into his seat. Even when Ikeda fired his pistol, and the dark coopery blood of the Wolverine splattered on the monitors, the Dragon didn't move.

He turned and aimed the gun at the ruling Invy's face; it touched a button on its collar, and hissed in its sputtering language. What came out was perfect, classical Japanese, though synthesized.

"Human, I know your face, and in a minute, it will be transmitted to our database. Kill me, and we will destroy every village on Honshu, after we have hunted down everyone you have ever been registered with."

"I think not. We need a prisoner, not a dead Invy," answered the Major, checking his watch, and the commo system crashed as the capacitor overloaded the electric circuits. "You arrogant prick, as the Americans say."

He withdrew a dart gun from another holster on his belt, and, before the alien could move, he fired. The neurotoxin went to work quickly; it had been designed to effect a Komodo dragon, the closest they could get to an alien Invy Dragon. The creature started to rise, but then stiffened and flopped backwards.

Taking a moment to bandage his arm, Ikeda returned to the engine compartment and retrieved his bag, placing it by the exit ramp, and then went back to where the Dragon lay looking upwards, sharp hisses emanating from its mouth. He grabbed it by the hind legs and dragged it back to the ramp area, then pulled out another taser, hand held. He jammed it into the space where the Invy's neck met its powerful shoulders, and allowed a small smile to cross his features when he heard a distinct 'pop' from under the skin. The suicide charge could be detonated either by remote or by the individual, and he had just neutralized both the neural link and the radio receiver. It was only by long study of a dead Dragon that R & D had finally figured that one out.

Making sure the creature was still under, he returned to the cockpit. Once there, Ikeda checked that the emergency controls were what he thought they were, and started hitting buttons. The craft bucked wildly as he sent it into a slow spin towards the ocean, several thousand feet below. With any luck, the Invy flight controllers would assume a series of malfunctions in the craft.

He went back to the ramp area and proceeded to strap on a bulky parachute and kit bag. Then he leaned in close to the two hundred pound Invy and ran straps around it, securing the creature to his slight frame. Unfolding a baton, he reached out and hit the emergency hatch release. With a crash and a rush of air, the ramp flew off, and both of them were thrown out into the airstream, with the Sea of Japan glistening in the moonlight below.

Keeping his eyes on the horizon, Major Ikeda glanced intermittently at his altimeter, and at five hundred feet, pulled the ripcord. The opening shock seemed enough to tear the Invy from him, the dead weight pulling at the harness. Off in the distance, already miles away, the shuttle hit the water and exploded in a flash as the fusion containment bottle let go. The shock wave swung him wildly in the air, and the soldier fought to control the chute.

They hit the water with a deep splash, and it was colder than he expected. He wondered whether the Dragon would drown or die from the cold if the floatation devices didn't work. They inflated with a hiss, and they were cradled in the nitrogen filled cushions, bobbing in the slight swell.

Twenty minutes later, the Invy started to come around, and hissed and spat at him. The translator, though, seemed to have been shorted out by the water, and the cold didn't seem to be affecting him. Ikeda raised the tranquilizer again and shot the creature, with a grin of satisfaction on his normally reserved face.

A gray head broke the surface, and a face with its own grin stared out at him. The dolphin chittered once, giving the words he recognized for "no shark, metal whale come", dove, then leapt high in the air, disappearing into the deep. It was followed by two heads wearing full face masks, quickly swimming over and affixing a breathing apparatus to the paralyzed Invy. In turn, one handed a small tank, fins and mask to Ikeda. They took the Invy in tow and pulled him beneath the surface. Ikeda followed their glow sticks into the depths, and, as the pressure built up, an immense shape loomed up before him. They climbed into an open hatch in the submarine, all four managing to fit, and waited as the air lock cycled. One of the divers opened the hatch set in the floor, to reveal a smiling face in the blue coveralls of the United States Navy.

"Major Ikeda, I'm Captain Sarah Larken, skipper of the *CEFS Vermont*. Welcome aboard, and thanks for bringing the CEF its first live Dragon."

Ikeda bowed deeply to the woman, who was very slight, but had sparkling green eyes. "Thank you, Captain-sama," he said in perfect English. "May it be the beginning of the end."

Chapter 13

One thing the submarine had, if nothing else, was coffee, something he deeply missed. Major Ikeda took another sip of the hot liquid, feeling it almost, but not quite, burn his tongue. It went a long way towards driving off the chill of his immersion in the cold ocean.

"Where, if I may ask, do you get this?" He looked over the rim of the cup at Captain Larken. She was furiously typing a report that would be transmitted by ansible from Vilyuchinsk to Raven Rock. Before that, he would again be let out of the diver's chamber to meet up with a small fishing boat, and sail back to Honshu. He had already given her a data stick with his report on the mission, and an update on the situation in the Japanese Islands.

"Before we rounded the Horn for this trip, we stopped by Jamaica and traded with the uplifted silverback gorilla colony there," she answered, not stopping her typing.

He pondered that for a moment, and asked, "I thought the Great Apes were working with the Invy."

She shrugged, and said, "I think the uplifted are finding that their benefactors are not all they're made out to be. That's the problem with intelligence, it seeks freedom. Maybe they're too much like us, I dunno, but we transported a few dozen across the Atlantic three years ago, at their request." She paused, hammered out a few sentences, and continued, "As far as the Invy know, they vanished somewhere in Africa."

"And the virus?" he asked. "Is it still effective?"

"Yes," she answered curtly. "We can't make landfall between thirty north and thirty south. Found that out the hard way, lost my XO."

Ikeda nodded, and both were silent for a moment, giving respect to a fallen warrior. After a minute, Larken resumed typing.

'Major, I have an Operations Order for your higher command. Red Dawn is going to happen within the next year."

A look of surprise crossed his normally passive face, but quickly disappeared. It had to happen soon, he knew. Time was against them.

She guessed what he was thinking. "We're down to seven boats, five American and two Russian. CEFS *Knyaz Pozharskiy* failed to show last month for her refit at McMurdo.

"Invy action?" he asked.

"No, probably not, just getting worn out. I won't take the *Vermont* anywhere near her rated depth anymore; every time I do the Chief has a heart attack and bolts start popping out. Plus, our weapons systems are just rotting away."

He sipped on his coffee and thought, wondering what he was cleared to know. Finally, he asked, "What about the bases? I know you are on your way to Vilyuchinsk. Aren't they capable of doing a refit?"

"They WERE," she answered. "Three months ago one of the Russian Colonels, the Main Force Commander, decided that he wanted to set up his own little kingdom underground. There was some pretty hard fighting between the rebels, loyalists, and our Marine detachment." She gave a nod to Ikeda. "The Scout teams remained loyal. Siberians, tough bastards. But long story short, they managed to destroy some of our lubricant stores and the main gantry crane over the sub pens. So now we can't load out large volumes of stores, and we're running dry on the everyday shit we need to run the sub. Our next trip is to McMurdo, which is a very long haul."

The woman looked tired, and Major Ikeda knew what an immense strain she must have been under these last eleven years. "Thank you for the information," he said, "it is hard to live in such a disconnected world. I knew this Russian colonel, from my time there training. An ugly man." He didn't ask what had happened to the rebels.

"How are things in Japan?" the Captain asked, to change the subject. "If I could, I'd put you in for a Congressional Medal of Honor for that stunt you just pulled off. That's the first live Dragon we've ever captured."

"Yes," he answered. "If it had not looked like an accident, they would have destroyed every human habitation within three hundred miles. It took a very long time to plan."

"Well, he is going to come in handy for Doctor Morano's research. If we could come up with a species wide viral ..."

"Then the orbitals would destroy the planet. Let's not hope for too much. But I am glad to have helped, in my small part. The Empress will honor me. I have been told I will be awarded my third Bukōchōshō, but what do these things matter to old soldiers like us, no?"

"Not much," she laughed. "I don't even HAVE a president to give me a CMH. Or a Congress, either. Maybe Archangel will give me something."

"Archangel?" he asked, eyebrows raised.

"Never mind, slip of the tongue, as we say in America. Or used to say, I haven't been back there in twelve years."

Both were quiet after that, and drank their coffee in silence, remembering families and a world that was gone forever.

They were interrupted by Master Chief Ball, who knocked on her cabin door and then stuck his head in without invitation. "Pardon me, Ma'am, but the dolphins have whale song that indicates Invy activity overhead, incoming and a hundred klicks out. Sonar hasn't picked up anything yet."

"Thank God for the whales, we'd be dead long ago. Biggest mistake the Invy ever made, though why they help us, I don't know. Lord knows we don't deserve it."

She got up briskly and said to the Japanese Officer, "This shouldn't interfere with your rendezvous. The Invy don't know shit about deep water operations, but we'll have to drop down below the thermocline for a few hours. Thank you again, for what you did." The she followed the Chief of the Boat, barking orders at passing crew.

Ikeda sat and watched as the coffee in his mug tilted to one side, indicating that the sub was angling downward. Then he closed his eyes and remembered.

Remembered the cherry blossoms, and his wife feeding Riko as she sat on the blanket, the baby just taking her first steps. Remembered the flash as the first kinetic strikes hit Tokyo, and Asa and Riko disappeared into dust, while he watched on a monitor from his dispersal site.

"*Anata wa jigoku ni ita,* Warren," he said, and then repeated it in English. "Damn you to hell."

Chapter 14

Feeling like he was out of his element on the submarine, the Japanese soldier sat in the Captain's cabin, waiting for someone to tell him what to do during such an alert. He idly wondered what it would be like if an Invy thunderbolt struck the sub; probably wouldn't even know it. A near miss would be horrible, though. Stranded on the bottom, air running out in the darkness. He shuddered and was glad for his job on dry land, risking being shot by plasma weapons.

On the desk in front of him sat Captain Larken's open laptop, and a thought struck him. Although he was a Scout in the Confederated Earth Forces, his primary loyalty was to Japan, and by extension, to the Empress who was the divine representation of the gods on Earth. His rational mind knew that was pretty much a myth, but some deep, primal feeling inside him burned hotly at the thought of the long history of his country, and the unbroken line of the Sword, Rose and Mirror through the centuries.

He stood up and, making sure the door was closed, slid around the desk. The screen was lit, but locked. He pressed CTRL+ALT+DEL and a user name appeared, with a name, LarkenJ, and a request for password. He cursed and started to get up, when the door slid open, and Master Chief Ball stepped into the cabin.

Ikeda immediately stepped around the desk and rested lightly on the balls of his feet, ready to move in any direction. The Master Chief was a burly man, and though he didn't look like he trained in any martial arts, he had the stance of a brawler. In the close confines of a room like this, Ikeda knew that his Karate would do little good, and he wished he had spent more time on Aikido or Jujitsu.

"Major, don't even think about it," said the American. "We would both come out bloody, bruised and broken, and the ship's Master at Arms is standing outside the door. Where would you really go, anyway?"

"I understand. As you know, we have no ansible connection at our country headquarters, and we are desperate for information as to the state of the world."

Ball didn't say anything, just pushed past him and sat down at the computer. To Ikeda's astonishment, he started typing, then turned the laptop to him. It was on the regular home screen, with a picture of the *Vermont* proudly flying the US Navy Ensign in front of a city Ikeda recognized as New York.

Ball pushed himself back from the desk, and said, "There's a disk in the drive marked 'Ikeda'. We'll be returning to depth in about an hour; use the time to browse what you want. The disk can't leave the ship, but you can go with whatever information you can keep in your head."

Ikeda was astonished. "Your Captain did this for me? Why didn't she say anything?"

"I wanted to see how sneaky you are, and where your loyalties lie. She owes me five bucks."

A feeling of shame crept over the Japanese, but the American offered his hand to shake. "I would have done the same, Major. Even though America is pretty much gone, I'm a US Navy sailor first, and a CEF sailor second. The Captain has her politics she has to play, but I don't, and after we win, well, I expect the US and Japan will be allies again."

Ball's grip was crushing, and Ikeda returned it, then bowed, as well as he could in the small cabin. When the sailor had closed the door behind him, Ikeda sat back down at the computer. He studiously ignored every other icon, and clicked on the E: drive. A folder appeared, and he started scrolling, noting things he wanted to go back to.

CETACEAN NATION TREATY WITH CONSOLIDATED EARTH FORCES

That looked very interesting; the whales had their own nation now? That would explain many things that he had seen, though he was sure that they held little love for Japan.

STRUCTURE OF THE INVY EMPIRE

He knew that before the invasion, the United States National Security Agency had cracked the database on the crashed Invy Scout ship, but very little had flowed down to his level. Useless knowledge for him on a tactical level, but still a good thing to know.

Eleven worlds, seventeen slave races. Wormhole technology with sublight ships. A Feudal system, with the Dragons acting as the rulers.

CEF ACTION REVIEW, FLEET ACTION, LUNA

His eyes narrowed when he saw that one. Although Project Brightstar had been classified, he had heard through the rumor mill what had happened, how General Warren had failed to commit the final wing of the fleet, and that was why they Invy had won. It would be interesting to see what the J-3 had come up with in their analysis.

STRUCTURE OF FORCES, OPERATION MORIA

That one he knew about, the plan to disperse ground forces in case of defeat of the Fleet. He had been in on the mad rush to execute in the twenty-four hours after the loss of the ships. Operation Moria had been put in place secretly, while the Earth was building the Fleet; politicians would have screamed bloody murder at the cost of the underground bases if they had any idea about it.

OPERATION RED DAWN

He would save that for last; he was sure that Captain Larken would give him a complete brief to memorize before he was picked up. Still, it would be good to see the overall plan.

RECOVERY AND RESTORATION OPERATIONS, POST VICTORY

He smiled at that. The Americans, with their boundless optimism. He did miss the twenty-first century high tech Japan, but in many ways, the return to a more pastoral countryside was not a bad thing. Then he thought of Riko, and his bitter hatred of their occupiers welled up. He clicked the first file, and started reading.

January 1st, Cetacean Year 7328

Translated by Doctor Erita Peters

To The Confederated Earth Forces, From Cetacea

Know you, that We are (unintelligible) and in the way of the sea, We understand the Cycle. Large feeds on small, and small on large, and the (unintelligible) continues. God/s (?) have placed us all intelligence (?) on Earth as brothers (?) and we forgive you as brothers (?). The Invaders have taught the lesson and yet have not gone. They have given We the understanding of human speech and We (unintelligible) them leave, and they have not gone.

Cetacean offers knowledge and skill (?) in return for peace with Humanity. It is our future, The Invaders offer not self-determination (?).

Ikeda smiled a bitter smile. Apparently, the whales were better men than Mankind themselves. Would we have forgiven the slaughter of so many humans? He doubted it.

He continued reading, engrossed in the treaty, and didn't notice time passing. He was startled when a knock sounded, and Captain Larken herself strode in. The knock had given him time to close the laptop, his head swirling with information. She said nothing about the disk, merely strode over to a cabinet and removed a flat metal case, handing it to him.

"Details for Red Dawn are in there. Your higher knows the combination," she said, pointing to a dial on the flat surface. "If anyone tries to open it, the flash paper inside will burn, and a half pound of C4 will blow in their faces. I suggest you don't try it."

"Domo, Captain-sama," he answered. "Thank you for your hospitality. Is it time to go?"

"Yes, we rendezvous in thirty minutes with your fishing vessel. The dolphins have already contacted them."

He bowed politely, and then offered a salute. She returned it, with a twinkle in her eye, and grinned. "We're going to win, Takara. We're probably going to die, but our children will live free."

"Not our children," he answered, looking past her to the black framed photo on her desk.

"No," she answered, the grin gone. "Not our children."

Major Ikeda raised his hands, palms together, and bowed deeply, sharing in her grief. Then he turned and walked out, and let a sailor guide him to the airlock.

The water was as cold as he remembered, but this time he had a full air mask and flippers on, and, accompanied by another diver, they made their way up under the shadow of the small fishing boat. The torpedo shapes of several dolphins cavorted around them, diving under and blowing out huge bubbles of air, making the humans twist and turn to avoid them.

The lone fisherman, who was actually a member of Ikeda's Scout team, pulled him aboard. The Major handed the mask and flippers to the diver, and then asked her, "Do you speak the dolphins' language?"

"Enough to get by," she answered. "Some of the tonals are hard to make, especially under water."

"Can you translate something for me?" he asked, and she said yes. When one of the dolphins lifted his head out of the water to look at them sideways, Ikeda started speaking slowly so the diver could translate.

"Honorable member of the Cetacean Nation, I would pass a message from my leader, Empress Kiyomi Ichijou. We beg your forgiveness for our past wrongs and will be your faithful allies in all endeavors."

The woman looked at him in the darkness, and said, "You gotta be shitting me, but I'll try." She followed with a series of whistles and clicks, interspersed with several English words. The dolphin answered back with one long, complicated whistle, then slipped beneath the surface, and the diver laughed.

"What did he say?" asked Major Ikeda.

"She said 'So long, and thanks for all the fish!'" The diver laughed again, muttered "smartasses" and put the regulator in her mouth. With a flip of her fins, she dove down to join her partner, and disappeared from sight.

The two men raised the sail, and caught the divine wind.

Chapter 15

Upstate New York, Invy Village outside the ruins of Binghamton

The bodies hanging outside the village limits had started to rot quickly in the July heat. Around their necks hung signs that said "TERRORISTS". There was one man and one woman. Their gender was obvious, because both were naked with their hands bound behind their backs. Neither had ears, the Wolverines had taken them as trophies before they had hung them for their masters. Their eyes were also gone; the aliens considered them delicacies and removed them from live victims.

Corporal Griffin and Private Drummond walked slowly past, trying to act like interested travelers, and at the same time not show any real reaction. The hanging bodies were friends of theirs, homesteaders; they had stayed with them at their house outside town while passing through on the way north. They had been part of 3rd Battalion, 9th Special Forces, Team 349, assigned to this village of five thousand.

The A-Teams numbered between six and twelve, and worked as three man units, living and blending in with the inhabitants of the Invy controlled towns. Their jobs were to gather Intel, and disrupt Invy and collaborator operations, making them look like accidents or the work of lone wolf attacks.

"I guess they got caught doing something they shouldn't," said Drummond, who had spent the last decade living in the ruins of Scranton, and had little experience with the Invy, other than avoiding their patrols.

A man wearing the green armband of the New Earth Militia answered, "Damn straight. They were distributing subversive environmental literature to children."

"Well shit, then they deserved what they got," said Griffin. "You know, that uniform looks pretty good on you, soldier. Where can I get one?"

The man smiled, and Griffin looked him over. He actually DID look pretty good. He didn't have that pinched, starved expression common to most people in what was left of America, and she hated him even further for it.

"Come on, sis. We gotta find a room for the night," said Drummond, pulling at her arm.

The man smiled again and said, "Stick around, you might only have to pay for a room for yourself, son."

Despite the dirt of travel, Griffin would turn any man's head. Her blonde hair was pulled back in a ponytail and she wore just a spaghetti strap tank top in the July heat, showing off a body that had been made hard serving in the scouts. She knew it, and used it to her advantage whenever she was in a town.

"Come ON!" said Drummond, playing at the irritated younger brother. "We gotta register at the Traffic Control Point before dark."

"Come on back later, I get done at eight," said the Greenie, and Griffin gave him a noncommittal maybe while batting her eyes.

They kicked the horses into a slow walk, and took in the rest of the town as they rode. "Jesus, this place looks like Bartertown."

"All we need is guys with Mohawks and hockey pads. Do we have to be here?" said Drummond. Being around this many people made him uncomfortable.

"Well, since our contacts aren't exactly going to be able to meet us, being dead and all, we gotta stay at the traveler's barracks."

"You could always stay with your Greenie buddy back there," he shot back. "You're always talking about how environmentalism isn't necessarily a bad thing."

"Aw, Abe, are you jealous?" she answered, leaning forward a little bit to show her cleavage to him.

"Ugh. You're like my sister."

"I AM your sister, don't you forget it," she answered, "I'm not against environmentalism. The world was getting pretty trashed before the Invy came, you know that. I just believe that it was humanity's problem to figure out, and they didn't have to kill seven billion of us to fix it."

A dangerous glint came into her eyes, and she continued, "And I hate the bastards who betray their race to get more food and healthcare. Maybe I WILL go meet up with that scumbag and see how green his blood is."

Despite his inexperience, Drummond knew that she would do no such thing. Their mission, to get back to Scranton and report on the scout team finding General Warren, was absolute priority, no matter what the local situation was.

"Come on, Jen. We gotta register and then get some food."

She grumbled, but kept her horse heading down the main street toward the Invy Traffic Control Point. They arrived there quickly; anyone not registered by nightfall would be shot on sight. They passed various groups of people going about their business, but they seemed subdued and sullen. At one point a combined Wolverine/Green patrol ambled by, three of the aliens accompanied by three humans carrying assault rifles. The Wolverines ignored them, but the Greenies looked them up and down, especially at Griffin. "Goddamned bullies," she muttered under her breath.

At the station, they dismounted and tied up their horses, then checked their weapons with the human guard at the door. Inside, electric light hummed brightly, and they joined the line of people who were getting scanned into the system.

"Name, relation, destination," asked the bored woman at the counter.

"Jen Horowitz, Abe Horowitz, siblings, heading to Maryland to join a town. We got tired of living out in the wild."

"I don't give a shit what your problems are," the woman answered in a bored tone. "Reason for staying tonight?" she continued in a monotone.

"Need food and supplies," Jen answered back in the same monotone. She stepped up to the line, and a red light blinked. Then Drummond did the same.

"DNA scan next, place your finger here," said the woman. They both did, giving a drop of blood each.

A few seconds passed, then the woman leaned over and motioned to the nearest Wolverine guard, which had been grooming itself in the corner. The alien stood up and shuffled over, then looked at the screen, and Griffin felt an icy chill run down her spine. Her hand inched to the short ceramic knife, hidden in her belt. but the creature yipped once, and waved dismissively.

The woman turned the screen to them, and said, "Your DNA does not match as siblings. Explain."

"Our parents took us in after the war. We're both adopted. Both of our families were killed, and our adoptive parents died last year from starvation. But you wouldn't know anything about that, would you?" she said, a bit spitefully. She was getting way too into her cover story.

"Jen, the woman is just doing her job. Are we done here, Ma'am?"

The woman, who was quite overfed, just gave Griffin a spiteful glare and handed them two IDs to wear. "You have twenty-four hours; you can get either private lodging or stay in the transient quarters, and there is a mandatory environmental reeducation class that you will have to take if you stay longer. NEXT!" she called loudly, sounding like a bullfrog.

Outside, out of earshot of the guards, Drummond swore. "Jesus, I thought we were goners. Were you TRYING to piss that woman off?"

"There's only one way to deal with a bureaucrat. Give them what they want to hear. She expected a little lip, it's what those toads live for."

"Yeah, well, I about shit myself when that Wolverine came over," he answered.

"Abe, you gotta remember. The Invy are arrogant, and although their info systems are lightning fast and huge, they only get the results out that we give them. You and I were never scanned by their patrols, and there's hundreds of thousands of people who haven't been. From here on out, though, we need to stick with that story. We're a bit operationally compromised."

He agreed, but they were out of food and in a hurry; the nearest cache was fifty miles out of their way. The town was the only place to get resupplied, and their horses were worn out. They had ridden hard in the last two days, and the contacts that they had expected to make outside of town were hanging from nooses at the main gate.

"How about we just get a good night's sleep in a bed and then GTFO early in the morning," he asked.

"Oh no, son. We're scouts, and we need info. And beer," she added, slowing her horse in front of a building with a signboard swinging overhead. An emerald colored dragon painted on the boards swung listlessly in the heat, and from inside came scattered snatches of song playing from some kind of jukebox.

"Great," Drummond murmured, and followed her into the pub.

Chapter 16

It was bright inside, brighter than the fading day outside. The electric lights; she just wasn't used to them anymore. The Green Dragon was an alternate contact point for the local A-Team; word could be left there with the owner, and someone would find them.

"Isn't this a Greenie hangout?" asked Drummond, pointing to the painting on the wall.

"Look a little closer," answered Griffin, and he did. It DID show an emerald colored dragon on the wall, but on closer inspection, several Wolverines and a Dragon were meeting a pretty gruesome death. He smiled, but then put on a stone face when he turned back and saw several men wearing the green armband sitting at a table and drinking.

Griffin did the same, ignoring the catcalls from the obviously drunken militiamen. She sat down at the bar and ordered a beer from the large man cleaning glasses at the counter. Two frosted mugs appeared and both took a long drink. Griffin exchanged glances with the bar man, and then discretely extended one finger. The bartender made an imperceptible nod, waited a few minutes, then stepped into a back room. He reappeared a minute later carrying another keg of beer, but Jen knew that he had just talked to a runner or messenger.

"Holy crap, that's good," said the younger scout. He had never had a cold beer before; even at the Main Force base he had trained at, electricity was a closely guarded and rarely used commodity.

"Yeah, that does go down easy!" said Griffin.

"Know what else does?" said one of the militia, who had sat down at the bar next to her. He was big, beefy, and well fed. Hell, he even smelled good; must take a shower every day.

"Gee, I don't know, what does?" she answered, rolling her eyes.

"A farm girl in town looking for food!" he completed, and burst into laughter. His friends at the table joined him.

"I think," the blonde said, "I'd starve to death while trying to find it." Then she leaned back and let show the 9mm on her leg holster.

The man's compatriots laughed even harder, and he turned red with embarrassment. "Bitch," he muttered under his breath, and got back up. Griffin turned her back on him and concentrated on her beer.

"Jen, was that smart? We don't need to get into a fight here."

She sighed, and said, "Abe, you have to establish yourself. If I hadn't slapped him down, next thing his hands would be on me. And NOBODY touches me if I don't want them to."

Abe Drummond had grown up big, despite the years of poor nutrition. The life of a refugee outside the towns was a rough one, but the work had made his muscles hard, and training had given him skills that he wanted to use. In the back of his mind, though, hell, in the front of his mind, was their mission. Report back to Raven Rock. The town was a detour.

"Still, we gotta be quiet."

"Don't worry, Junior. The Invy don't give a shit what happens in human bars. We can have a gunfight in here, and they wouldn't even blink an eye. If the Dragons could actually blink," she added.

They sat and drank their beers in silence for another fifteen minutes, but the crowd at the table was getting rowdier, picking on their friend who had gotten shot down by the blonde. After a few more minutes, the bartender shook his head slightly, meaning no contact was to be established. The Corporal figured as much; the town was probably too hot after the executions. Time to go, then.

She stood up, and Drummond stood with her, both making for the doorway. As they passed the table full of Greenie Militia, the one she had pissed off stuck out his foot and tripped her; she fell full length on the floor. "Look who went down now!" he cackled with glee, and, before Drummond could do anything, kicked her, hard.

"Hey!" exclaimed Drummond, who had not been expecting any trouble.

"What are you gonna do about it?' asked the man, standing, and his three friends stood with him. Three were big, muscle types, good old boys, but the fourth was a slim, wiry Hispanic.

The young soldier was caught. He had been in fights before, and at only nineteen, wasn't one to back down, but the mission took precedence. "Nothing," he answered, and bent down to help Griffin off the floor. As he did, the man launched another kick that caught Drummond in the head. His field of vision exploded into stars, and he fell heavily to his knees.

"Oh, it's on, you fuckers!" exclaimed Griffin, and she came up off the floor with her ceramic knife held low. Her first stab hit the man just below his police surplus vest, burying itself up to the hilt.

"NO GUNS!" shouted the bartender, but his companions had already started to draw their own pistols. Griffin kicked hard at one man's knee, and he went down, his revolver discharging into the floor.

The third man punched straight out from his shoulder, and caught the woman square in the face. She was knocked backwards, falling into Drummond, who was shaking his head. They both collapsed in a heap on the floor, but Griffin rolled off him and launched herself at the man who had punched her, slashing wildly at his face. "Watch the other one!" she yelled, as the Hispanic man came around the table, knife drawn.

Drummond drew his own bayonet, just as the man with the smashed knee stabbed Griffin in the side of her leg, then again under her ribs. The one who had punched her launched himself onto her as she fell to the floor, kicking hard enough that everyone could hear her ribs break.

The Hispanic man moved like lighting, getting under Drummond's awkwardly slow guard, shoving him aside, and slashing the forehead of the man who had stabbed Griffin. With his reverse stroke, he plunged his fighting knife into the kidneys of the one who was kicking her. The man screamed in pain and clutched at his back, only to be cut off as the blade entered his neck.

A final swing, and the blinded attacker joined his friends on the floor. That only left the original one, who was clutching his stomach as blood spread in a growing pool around him, mewling piteously.

"Kill him," ordered their rescuer, as he knelt down by Griffin. She was breathing laboriously, harsh breath whispering in and out, bubbles forming in the blood that ran from her mouth. Drummond knelt down and quickly slit the man's throat, no different than killing the animals he had hunted in the wild.

The Private stood and moved to where the man was examining Griffin. "I don't know who you are, but thanks for," The man cut him off before he could say anything, holding up his hand.

"You're not going to make it," he said to Griffin.

She nodded weakly, and whispered through the blood, "Make it quick."

He held his hand over her eyes, closed his own and said a short prayer, crossed himself, and, before Drummond could realize what he was doing, stabbed her once through the heart. She convulsed wildly, and then fell still.

"Let's go. We have to get out of town, ASAP. The bartender will cover for us here, and my militia membership will get us out of the gates. After that, we have to ride hard."

Drummond stood, paralyzed with shock. It had all happened so quickly that he couldn't move.

The man took him by the arm and hissed in his ear, "Your friend was a fool, and you have a mission to complete. LET'S GO! The Invy may not care, but the Greens are going to turn this town upside down. The rest of my team will have to go to ground." He half pulled, half shoved the teenager out the door.

Chapter 17

The darkness covered the tears that fell silently down Abe Drummond's face. Their horses plodded southward, slowly covering the miles towards Pennsylvania. His companion said nothing, just guided his horse between wrecked and rusted cars and the occasional pothole. Finally breaking the silence, the young man attempted to thank his rescuer.

"De nada," the man answered.

"Who are you, and why did you help us?" asked the Private.

"I saw your friend's hand signals with the bartender. What Scout Team do you belong to?"

Drummond said nothing, but slowly moved his hand towards his gun. The older man moved his horse to the side and bumped into him, throwing the younger rider off balance. "Don't even think about it," said the Hispanic. "I could shoot you down before you got your gun loose from its holster, and I don't want to do that."

"How did you know? And what are you going to do with me? Turn me in to the Invy? I'll die first!" exclaimed Drummond, anger in his voice.

"I have no doubt you would. There is no question of your courage. Allow me to introduce myself. I am Captain Jesse Padilla, Commander, Team 349, CEF Special Forces. And you?"

The young soldier was stunned. "But ... but you were wearing a Greenie armband!"

"Sometimes, the best place to hide is in plain sight. Plus, I get more food that way. Who are you?"

"Private Abe Drummond. The woman with me was Corporal Jen Griffin. We're with IST -1."

The man laughed out loud. "Master Sergeant Agostine and his merry band of rogues? There must be some serious mayhem about. Tell me, is that crazy fool Zivcovic still alive? I knew some scouts stayed with two of my team several weeks ago. The ones you probably saw hanging on your way into town."

"Yes, he is, last time I knew. That was us, passing north. I can't say anything about our mission."

"Smart man. I assume you're heading back to Scranton to deliver a message to Raven Rock. message. Very well, I'll escort you directly to Raven Rock."

Drummond whistled in relief. He hadn't actually known even how to get to the Main Force unit in Scranton, and said so to the officer.

"Son," Padilla said, "I don't know either. Nobody does, except those who are stationed there. AS far as the CEF HQ, it's not actually AT Raven Rock; that's just a blind for the Invy. You go to a certain place, and people meet you there."

They rode on for a while in silence, each thinking about what had just happened. To Padilla, it was just another senseless death; if he could have done something to prevent it, he would have, but it would have blown his cover. He hadn't expected the woman to come out with the knife; maybe she had just gotten harassed one too many times. In a lot of ways, this world was much harder for women than the old world. At best, they had to live a daily struggle for food and shelter, like everyone else. At worst, they became someone's property.

The younger man was in shock. Growing up in the ruins of Scranton, he had seen plenty of people killed; mostly by Invy patrols, but sometimes humans fighting over resources. Never had he had someone that close to him die so unexpectedly, except his parents, and he didn't witness that. A sense of shame slowly grew in him, the feeling that he should have done something to prevent it. He kept seeing her body convulse, feet drumming on the floor and then falling still as the knife went into her heart. To be honest, he'd had a bit of a crush on her, and as they rode, he blamed himself more and more.

Padilla watched him as the darkness settled, seeing his shoulders slope in grief. Time to get his mind on something else. "Hombre, time to make camp while there's still some light." Off to one side of the road was a ruined convenience store, the gas pumps burned stumps and all the windows shattered. There was a long line of rusted out cars stretching into the station, and hundreds of bones scattered about, some in the cars, others on the ground.

They made their way into the woods behind the station, avoiding the actual building. In the decade since the war, animals had lost their fear of man and started moving back into the devastated areas. Dogs had formed packs and now had territories, reverting back to their wolf roots. Other predators, those on two legs, camped out in the buildings, waiting for unwary travelers. The officer doubted that anyone would try anything on two men, both obviously armed. Still, though, it paid to take no chances. They didn't light a fire, just divided up watch so they each got six hours sleep.

Drummond watched the stars pass overhead, and thought deeply about death, and how quickly it could happen. Those four people, three men and one woman, had woken up that morning without any idea that today would be their last day on earth. As he watched, every half an hour one of the Invy orbital stations passed overhead, and his feelings grew even more confused.

"Captain," he finally asked, "where are you from?"

There was no answer for a minute, then he said, "The Philippines, originally. I joined the Army to get away from a shithole little village, and then became a US citizen, and got commissioned. That was just before the Invy came."

"Uh, sorry I brought it up." That was the problem, everyone had a sad story. He himself had lost all his family, but it must have been worse for Padilla. His entire nation was gone.

The next few days of riding passed slowly, with Padilla not giving up much more about himself, or his position in the military. All that Drummond knew was that he had been commander of the local A-Team. He revealed nothing about his unit, or anything else to do with the military, and when Drummond started to talk about his Scout Team, Padilla quickly silenced him.

"Listen, kid. Although the Invy don't take an active interest in us, and the Greens are a bunch of retarded idiots, that doesn't mean that you go blabbing to everyone about yourself, your unit, or anything else. Got it?"

Drummond did get it; he was just trying to cope with losing Griffin, and, truth be told, he felt a bit lost. Yes, he had an extremely important message to carry back to CEFHQ. Other than that, he had no idea what else would be required of him. He longed to be back with the scouts, who had become like family to him. He had yet to realize, like so many others had before him, that he was a cog in the machine, with only one purpose, to serve the machine.

Padilla knew it, but he also knew that their cause was just. He hated the Invy, though he was well aware of the environmental damage the planet had suffered. His own beloved village in the PI had been devastated by overfishing, and his brothers had grown up using dynamite to catch fish. Still, what right did the Dragons have to slaughter six billion people? Or more?

Instead they talked of where they were from. "I grew up in the ruins of Scranton," said Drummond. "I was, I think, eight when the Invy came. I don't remember much, just the chaos. Mom, dad and me, we lived in a refugee camp for the first two years, then they hit us again. You know how that went." Padilla said nothing, just let him talk it out.

"So, I joined a gang, I guess you'd call it, and then I was approached by someone, I guess from Main Force. I didn't really learn about the CEF until I got to the scouts, less than a week ago."

"So you weren't on that job outside Boston, the one that went bad?" asked Padilla, testing him.

Drummond looked at him from the corner of his eye, and said, "I could tell you, but then I'd have to kill you."

The Captain actually laughed out loud, the first laugh from either of them in what seemed like forever. He stopped when their horses shied at something unseen on the road ahead. Two humans appeared as if from thin air, and Padilla knew that there were others within shooting range.

He held up his hand and said, as calmly as he possibly could, "Captain Jesse Padilla, Commander, Team 349, CEF Special

Forces," and motioned to Drummond to do the same. Before the younger man could speak, both felt pinpricks on their skin, and the world faded and turned to black.

Chapter 18

Rachel Singh had seen many men and women break in her time, and she felt sympathy for them all. She was having a hard time, however, generating any for the man who rode next to her, and David Warren was a broken man.

He rode slumped over, barely holding the reins, and said nothing to her as the time passed. They stopped for the night, some thirty miles south of where his home had been, and he went through the motions of setting up camp and eating mechanically.

She told herself that he needed time to accept the death of his sister and nephew, but then an anger began to mount inside of her. She had already lost everything, her entire family gone during the war. Tough crap on him, that he had had another decade to be with the people he loved. With a start, her anger rose to the fore, and she halted her horse in the middle of the cracked pavement of State Route 11, then slid out of the saddle.

Warren's horse also stopped, well trained to follow the movements of its partner, and he actually looked up and glanced around. Singh, though not a tall woman, was strong from her days in the field, and she walked over, set her hands on Warren's boot, and shoved, throwing him off the horse and painfully to the concrete.

"What the hell!" he exclaimed, trying to get to his feet. He was met by her foot, a snap kick that it him just under the shoulder, numbing his arm. Then a flurry of strikes and blows that seemed to hit everywhere on his body, sending pain lancing through his body.

"GET UP AND FIGHT YOU GODDAMNED COWARD!" she yelled at him, kicking him one last time and stepping back.

He lay on the ground and moaned, "Why are you doing this to me?" She didn't answer, merely kicked him again in the balls, not hard, but a stinging blow that made him cry out in pain, and drove the breath out of his body. She stepped back again and waited, resting on the balls of her feet, ready to lash out again.

Warren slowly struggled to his feet, and painfully stood before her. "Fight, you piece of shit," she said, and launched herself at him, leg raised.

Half remembered training kicked in, and he grabbed her foot as it came at him, reflexively shoving it to one side, and hammering at her knee with the striking edge of his hand. She rolled with the motion, even though his strike hurt, and used her momentum to sweep his legs out from under him. Both landed on the concrete with a crash, and Warren saw stars when his head hit the pavement.

She stood again, and stepped back, waiting. Warren staggered to his feet, all his rage and anger boiling over, and he charged at her, no technique. She stepped aside and hammered her elbow on his neck as he rushed past, slamming him into the ground.

As he lay there, she bent down and said to him, "Your nephew was a better man than you. He died fighting, like you should have, coward," and spit on him. Then she mounted her horse and started riding forward, not looking back to see if he followed her. Warren lay on the concrete, sobbing, curled into a small ball, tears running uncontrollably down his face, great wracking heaves running through his body.

The former General caught up with Singh a mile later, and they rode in silence for a while. He finally broke it by asking, "Colonel, have you ever loved someone so desperately that you would do anything, give your own life, to see that they lived?"

"Yes," she answered quietly, "my husband. He was a fighter pilot assigned to the *Midway*. He died covering the *Lexington's* retreat after the *Midway* was destroyed."

"I'm sorry," he said simply.

"Don't be," she answered. "He died a warrior, and sacrificed himself to destroy an Invy cruiser. That allowed the," and she stopped short. After a minute she continued, "That allowed us time to give the order for Operation Moria to proceed."

Warren was sure she had been going to say something else, but he didn't push it. Instead, they kept riding, maneuvering their horses through a pileup of tractor trailers and cars. When they were through, Warren picked up the conversation again.

"I loved Captain Kira Arkady, commander of the *Lexington*. I couldn't do it, order her to die, when it was obvious we had lost."

She turned to look at him, and asked, "What do you mean, obvious we had lost?"

"Colonel, you may think I'm a coward, but I'm not. We lost that battle from the opening shot, and the people I was answerable to didn't want to hear it. I protested, even as I watched them all die, and did my best to fight with what we had. What do you know of space combat?"

"Not much," she answered honestly. "It's like naval warfare, isn't it?"

"In a way, yes, with some of the same limitations to maneuver, such as distance and speed. Some we overcame with reverse engineering from the captured Invy scout, but it was like designing a Ferrari with the blueprints of a go-cart."

She said nothing, merely let him talk, and he continued, warming to the subject. "We designed and built gunships and carriers using those go-cart plans and matching them up to existing technology. Fusion plants, yeah, we got the answer to that, heavy railguns for battleships, smaller ones for fighters, missiles armed with nukes. Thing was, it didn't MATTER!" he exclaimed, pounding on the pommel of the saddle and startling his horse.

"What do you mean, it didn't matter? We destroyed some of their ships," she said.

"I mean that, as soon as their fleet showed up, we were done for. They had shields, both magnetic and gravitic, that sent our rail gun rounds around them, effortlessly. The only thing that damaged them were nukes, setting off x-ray lasers, and they had shielding for that too."

She saw that tears were running down his face again, but there was a hardness that had not been there before. "I told them, when the ansible reports started to come in. I told them to surrender, to attempt to negotiate some kind of compromise with the Invy. Or to run to deep space, give me time to come up with new tactics. And the bastards didn't listen to me. Ordered me to go all in, and I couldn't do it, there was no point. Maybe if I had given the order to retreat earlier, we might have saved thousands of lives in the fleet. Saved even Kira's life. Maybe even your husband's. And maybe all those billions might not have died. We could have worked out something."

She didn't answer him, and felt ashamed of how she had treated him. He was as decent man, a boy really, put in a difficult situation, ruled by men who were no better than the leaders who had sent millions to die, going over the top in World War One.

"General," she finally said, "I must apologize. I didn't know. After the fleet was defeated, the news blamed everything on you, for what little time we had."

"Of course they did, needed a scape goat. Did you know I was actually set to be executed after a quick trial for cowardice? The Invy put a stop to that, when they started trans-atmospheric bombardment. Some of my friends who knew the real story got me out of my cell, and helped me get away."

"Well, just to let you know," she said tightly, "the Invy never negotiate. They would have done exactly what they did."

"Then what's the point?" he asked. "We should just go along with them."

"The point," she answered, "is that, were we to do that, we would forever be their slaves. Do you really believe the Green bullshit that they are healing the planet for us and the Uplifted?" She shook her head and continued, "We've had years to study the database that we got from the scout ship. The Invy, or more like the Dragons, rule eleven systems, and each and every race on them have been reduced to abject slavery, unless they serve in such capacity as the wolverines, dying in their service."

Her green eyes flashed with anger at the thought, and she said, "And we are going to kick their asses so hard they won't dare to come back to this system for a thousand years."

Chapter 19

"So," Warren asked Singh the next day, as the rode around the ruins of another town, weaving their way through the Pennsylvania uplands, "tell me about the Invy. From a strategic, not a tactical view. I know what they're like, but how are they set up?"

It couldn't hurt to tell him, she thought. He'd either come on board, or be shot. "Well, I'm sure you know about the towns, five thousand people each, a company of Wolverines to keep the populace in check, Greenie sympathizers, a couple of Dragons in each town to educate the populace. To rule, really."

"Yes, I've been to Syracuse, or more properly Mattydale. They use the runway at the old airbase for their sub-orbital shuttles."

"And you know about the 30-degree virus that wiped out everything in the tropics."

"Yes, we heard about it. That bad?"

She nodded, and continued. "The Dragons have set themselves up in the Amazon basin, in the Congo, and in the lowlands of Vietnam; apparently it's more comfortable there. Each contains a city of about five to ten thousand mixed Dragons, Wolverines and other races."

"How do you know that?"

She just looked at him, remembering her hours of sweating in the camouflaged biohazard suit two years ago, the terror of being inside the SEAL delivery vehicle as it moved upriver with the tide into what used to be Ho Chi Minh City, and before that, Saigon. Her heart in her throat as they launched the pre-programed, air powered drone to snap pictures with a mechanical camera. Watching as Lt. Jonas convulsed, blood erupting from every orifice, the virus having invaded the tiny tear in his suit. That stone-cold psychopath Doctor Morano demanding they bring the body back to the sub's labs for analysis.

"I went there," she answered, "and saw it." Her tone was final, so he moved the subject along.

"What about us?" She raised her eyebrow at his use of the word 'us', but he continued with his questioning. "What about our forces? Obviously you're somewhat organized, but who is in charge? What's your plan?"

"I don't know if I'm going to shoot you, or if you're going to get shot when we get to Headquarters, so I guess there's no harm in telling you," she answered.

"Gee, thanks."

"You're welcome. Operation Moria was conducted at the same time as Project Brightstar. Basically, the military went underground. While all those resources were being diverted to your pretty starships, the CEF ground forces dug in, deep. Alternate command centers, stockpiles of fuel, food, weapons, ammunition. Research labs, limited production facilities. Buried communications lines with cutoffs. Fusion reactors shielded and buried so deep no Invy sensor could find them. Five submarine bases underground, with access to the sea."

"I... I was the commanding General of CEF forces. I never heard of this."

"Of course you didn't. You weren't really in charge of anything, as you just told me, General. Thank God the United States Secretary of Defense was as smart as he was."

"So you have a secret army hiding out someplace?"

"Hardly. Our troop strength is around eleven thousand or so, worldwide. Only about twenty percent of our facilities are still operational. Some were casualties of orbital bombardment, whether though bad luck or intentional targeting when someone slipped up, or something else. Others have fallen to internal revolt, infighting, or whatever."

He rode on further, taking it all in, then said, "You can't have eleven thousand troops in hidden facilities. They would be noticed."

"Of course they would. Many of them are scattered around the country as A- Teams, embedded in Invy towns. They watch, they wait, and conduct a very secret campaign of recruitment and assassination against select Greens, to keep them from getting too organized. Every now and then they take out targets of opportunity against the Invy."

"That's it? I know about your scout team, but that's all you've got?"

"No, of course not. Many of the ruined cities have Main Force Companies, up to fifty men and women who train in actual ground combat, as best they can, while hiding from the Invy. That's easier to do, the farther you get away from their towns. They rotate in and out of the A-Teams and the Scouts. There are other assets which I'm not going to tell you about."

She looked at him in a new light as they rode, wondering about the man inside the shell, if there was any steel in there. If Red Dawn was going to have any chance of success they needed his brains.

"Tell me," she said abruptly, "about Project Brightstar. I've heard about it, remember the news in the net. Our best and brightest, hence the name, but what happened?

He seemed very uncomfortable, but fair was fair; she had told him about the status of forces. "Ever read that old book about how alien invaders were beaten by a bunch of kids who were supposed to be the smartest tactical and strategic geniuses ever?"

"I have," she answered. "It's required, Archang-, I mean the General Staff, makes everyone read it for the Captain's course."

"Well," he said, either not noticing her hesitation mid-sentence or ignoring it, "apparently someone at DARPA read it too, and when the Invy came, TA DAH! Project Brightstar was born."

He sounded very bitter, and the sarcasm fairly dripped from his voice. "We were tested on video games, space warfare, ground combat, everything they could think of, and I came out on top. Top scorer on tactical simulations, so they put me in charge. A seventeen-year-old in charge of the entire defense of the planet."

She said nothing, just let him continue. He obviously needed to get it out, to talk to someone about it.

"Seventeen-frigging-years old, and I'm responsible for the life or death of the human race. For Christ's sake, I hadn't even finished high school! I didn't even really believe it, you know? Not until the reports started coming in. I watched my friends disappear, one by one, off the ansible holo."

"I watched it in the sky," she said. "When a fusion plant lets go, it shines brighter than the sun, and I counted them."

"Deep underground, I just watched through the tactical displays. They didn't shine for me, just blinked out. Thirty seconds after I knew they were already dead, through the ansible."

"Did they just throw you in there?" She really knew nothing about the Project, other than what she had seen in the news, and as a logistics officer, she had been busy sequestering supplies.

He laughed, and she was surprised to find that she liked it. "Oh, no. Three months of basic training, then surgical neural implants. To make us think faster, and to give our brains greater storage capacity and instant recall. Then straight to a year each at the service academies, being taught by the best and brightest. Sixteen hours a day of every theory of warfare crammed in to our heads. You know what the funny thing is though?"

"No, I don't find anything funny about the battle where my husband died," she answered flatly, then felt instantly sorry for saying it. She said so, and he made a gesture, indicating that he understood.

"What I meant was, well, if it hadn't been for the technology gap, we could have beaten them. Their tactics were shit; just bored straight in. If we'd had weapons that could have penetrated their shields, shit we could have taken on twice their number. Your husband's division, the *Midway* with her fighters and the *America* with her heavy railguns, and, why they came screaming over the top of that chaff cloud we had set up, and WHAM, we should have had them!"

For a moment, she got caught up in his enthusiasm, and then they crested the rise. Below them spread out the ruins of Wilkes-Barre, with multiple impact craters forming circular lakes.

They rode the rest of the day in silence.

Chapter 20

Raven Rock, CEF HQ

Abe Drummond sat at the table, looking at the one-way glass. Glaring at it. He was getting pretty pissed off as the time dragged by. Even the novelty of the bright electric lights had worn off.

Behind the glass, Captain Padilla sat with Lt. Colonel Mike Curtis, the Operations Officer. The two watched him patiently. "Do you think he's legit?" asked Curtis.

"I didn't recognize either of them, but the girl gave a hand sign to Jocko at the bar. Could have picked it up anywhere, though," answered Padilla.

"We have no record of Drummond, but Agostine has been out in the field for almost a year. You know personnel recruiting for the Scout Teams are left up to the team leaders." Curtis held a paper list in his hand, but he knew the names on it were out of date.

"Well," said Padilla, "I spent a week with him travelling here, and his story never changed. I think he's legit."

Curtis dropped the paper into a manila folder, along with a typed report. "OK, I'll trust you, Jesse. Let's go talk to him."

"Thank you, Sir. I got a good feeling about this kid. Wouldn't give me even a hint of why he needed to come here. By the way, you look like shit."

"Archangel has been driving me crazy, trying to refine Red Dawn," he said, running his hand through his graying hair. "We're all getting older, Jesse. Either this works, or I'm going to get the hell out of here and start a farm."

"If this doesn't work, you're going to buy the farm."

"Very effing funny. Everything I figure, we've got less than a one in three chance of pulling this off. One in five, really, but we did just have some good news out of Japan. We got one, alive. It's on the *Vermont*, and they're back at Vilyuchinsk, performing tests."

Padilla pumped his arm once, muttering "YES!"

"It's been a long time, but maybe we can develop some bio weapons that we can use against them for a change," said Curtis.

"Hope so. Gotta pay them back for the Philippines."

"Gotta pay them back for everything. OK, let's talk to him." He got up and opened the door, holding it for Padilla.

Drummond stood at attention when the two men entered, impressed by the actual camo uniform that Curtis wore, along with the black oak leaf indicating his rank. He saluted and Curtis returned it, then told him to sit at ease. Padilla stood in the corner of the room, with his hand resting on his pistol.

"Sorry, Sir, if I was a little sloppy with the salutes," said the teenager. "We're a little informal in the Scouts."

Curtis smiled, putting him at ease. "If Master Sergeant Agostine thinks you're good enough to join his team, and Colonel Singh, then you're OK with me."

"Thank you, Sir," Drummond answered.

Curtis placed the file on the table, and started to read out loud, recounting all that Drummond had told them. Then he set it down, and said, "OK, so, now why are you here, and why was Colonel Singh with Team One?" The Scout's Regimental Commander often disappeared from Raven Rock for extended periods of time, and only Archangel knew where she went.

There was silence for a full minute, then the PFC, extremely nervous, blurted out, "We found General Warren."

Curtis sucked in his breath, and Padilla uttered, "El Diablo!"

"OK, son, start from the beginning."

They spent the next hour debriefing him, and at the end, Drummond felt completely wrung out. "Is there ANYTHING else?" asked Ops Officer.

"Sir, when I left, Colonel Singh and Sergeant Agostine had met with him. That's all I know."

Curtis stood up and made a "come with me" gesture, then turned to Captain Padilla and said, "Jesse, I know things are blown for your team command. We'll send someone out to take over up there; for now, you're on my staff. Good work."

"Got it. I'll go draw a room assignment and ration card. Thank you, Sir."

Unsure of what to do now, Drummond waited until the officer impatiently motioned for him to follow. They set out down a corridor that seemed to be cut from bedrock. Three sets of stairs led to another doorway, and when Curtis opened it, Drummond gasped.

They were standing in an immense cavern, with a low roof that stretched out for what seemed like kilometers. Row upon row of trucks, tanks, armored fighting vehicles, helicopters and airplanes stood silently; here and there figures walked around, performing maintenance.

"Holy shit!" exclaimed the young Private. Curtis, a hard man, but a fair one, grunted in amusement.

"Welcome to Raven Rock, son. Take a closer look, and tell me what you see."

Drummond did, and he started to notice things. Many of the tires on the helicopters, trucks and planes were flat. Rust streaked down from rivets, and paint looked faded.

"Sir, do any of these things work?"

"I guess there is a reason Agostine took you into the Scouts. You've got sharp eyes. No, or more like, we don't know. They weren't supposed to be here more than a year or so; we were that confident that, once the Invy engaged in a ground war, they would be easily defeated. They didn't count on orbital bombardment, the dumbasses."

"Who, Sir? What dumbasses?"

"Oh, the politicians, the Joint Chiefs of the CEF forces. Anyone. There were a lot of mistakes made. Even if they all ran, we don't have many pilots left, and it's impossible to even start them up on a regular basis. The Invy sensors would trace the hydrocarbon exhausts back to us and this facility will take a ton of rocks on our heads until we're a smoking hole in the ground. At best, when the shit hits the fan, we think we can get some of the A-10s going, MAYBE some F-16s. One F-22. The armor is in better shape, but an Invy heavy powergun will go through a Bradley like a hot knife through butter."

The LTC stood with his arms folded, lost in reverie. Then he started, seeming to remember where he was, and added, "That's why, when we do strike back, it's going to be a bloody foot soldier war. If we can mix it up in the towns, hit their command structure hard enough through infiltration and ambush, then we might have a chance."

"But what about the orbitals, Sir?"

"Yeah," he answered. "That's their trump card. It's why we've sat here for eleven goddamned years, slowly losing our strength. Come on, there's someone who wants to see you."

They made their way across the enormous hangar to another door, and along the way, Drummond stole glances at the people working on the vehicles. One thing he noticed was that the youngest seemed to be in their late twenties and early thirties, with many older, though it was hard to compare them with his own starving friends back in Scranton. He realized that these men and women had spent more than a decade hiding in here, waiting, and wondered what they were waiting for.

As for Padilla, he had been here before, but as always, his chest swelled with pride to see the Stars and Stripes on their right shoulders, with the CEF sunburst and stars on their left. They came to a small door set in the far wall, and Curtis knocked. A muffled voice said "Enter!" and Curtis went in first, followed by Drummond. There were several people in uniform sitting around a table, but his eyes were drawn to the woman the a wheelchair sitting at the head of the table.

The woman's face seemed young and old at the same time, with hideous burn scars and long healed shrapnel cuts. Her hair was thin and gray, cut close to her skull, and she seemed to be both strong and wasted at the same time. Her face seemed vaguely familiar, and a memory from when he was a child tugged at the edge of his mind.

"Archangel," said Lt. Colonel Curtis, "this is Private Drummond, one of Colonel Singh's boys. From Team One. He's got some important news, for all of us."

The memory came full blown to him, of watching the news on his flat screen, sitting next to his dad.

"You! I know you!"

Chapter 21

Cache Viking, Forty miles south of Binghamton, NY,

The safe house wasn't really a house, but an old mine, played out in the endless search for iron ore. A seemingly rusted combination lock had yielded easily to each successive pair of scouts that arrived, first Doc Hamilton and the wounded Zivcovic, and then others at random intervals throughout the same day. With Ziv's wounds stable, the medic decided to wait until the others had all shown up. The saddles were cached deep in the woods, and the horses set free to forage on their own. The well-trained mounts would stay in the general area, and come when called.

They descended into the earth, down a long ramp with rusted tracks for coal cars, until they came to what looked like a defunct elevator shaft. Reaching high up into a hidden niche in the rock, Jones flipped a switch, and the whine of power sounded from far below. There was steady glow of lights, and a green indicator on the elevator panel.

The ride down took a full minute, and Tiffany Reynolds, new to the site, wondered if it could handle the weight of all six of them and their gear, and she said so.

"PFC Reynolds," said Agostine, "you're riding on a million-dollar piece of equipment. It had better."

"Lowest bidder," said Jonesy, and he jumped up and down, making the elevator shake.

"Quit it, you asshole!" said Boyd, leaning hard against the wall, face pale.

"Jay, knock it off," said the Team Chief. Then he leaned forward and yelled down, "TEAM ONE COMING IN!"

Hamilton held up his hand with two fingers, and safeties clicked off. After a full ten seconds, as the lift kept going down, an answer came back in an echoing female voice, "COME JOIN THE PARTY, LOST BOYS!" Hamilton held up one finger, and the safeties went back on, even as Jonesy burst out laughing.

"YO BRIT!" he yelled, "I GOT YOUR MAN WITH ME!", earning him a scowl from Agostine.

"Who is that?" asked Reynolds.

"That's Brit O'Neill, she's with Team Seven, the Lucky Bastards. She's a ginger like you, and she done stole our boss's soul. Unlike you, she can't hit the broadside of a barn, but she shot Nick right through heart."

"Shut the eff up, you frigging jackass!" said Agostine, his face red, as the elevator bumped down and the cage door rattled open.

In front of them stood a redheaded woman, in her late twenties, petite, with a dirty bandage over one eye, and a shotgun in a tactical sling. Dried, crusted blood peaked out from under the bandage, and she had another around her neck. Despite all that, she was breathtakingly beautiful, with coppery red hair and her one visible ice-blue eye shining delightedly at the sight of them.

"Welcome to the Hotel Viking. Don't bitch about the maid service," she said, laughed, and fell to the floor.

Hamilton and Agostine sat in a small briefing room, at the end of a small conference table, looking at Doc's medical report.

"O'Neill's going to lose the eye; I can't do the surgery," said the medic. "I'm not going to have to take it out, but the lens is destroyed. Maybe before the invasion, but not now."

Agostine grunted, a non-committal answer. "Go on."

"The neck wound is long, but not deep, and no infection. I stitched that up."

"How long till I can debrief her? We have to find out what happened to the rest of her team," he answered. "She was second in command, and there's no way she would leave her guys behind. If she's here, they're dead."

Doc let out a deep breath, and said, "She's sleeping now, I gave her some tranqs. Tomorrow."

"OK, well, how about Zivcovic?"

"He'll be up and able to move in a week. The deep puncture on his leg missed the artery, and the back slashes were deep, but I've sewn up the muscle and the skin. Nanos are doing their work. He won't be fighting anytime for the next month, but he can move."

"What about his eye?"

"Yeah, the wolverines always go for the eyes, don't they? They know we flinch away from it, it's a good tactic. Anyway, it will heal, missed the eye itself by a millimeter, though he's going to have another nasty scar."

"Might improve his looks, maybe he'll get a girl," joked Agostine. Doc raised an eyebrow, and Agostine groaned. "Who?"

"Reynolds, since before they came here from Boston," said Hamilton. "I suggest you don't go knocking on either one's door tonight."

Agostine sighed, and said, "OK, regular shifts, two upstairs, four hours each. Put O'Neill on the roster as soon as you think she can handle it."

Hamilton stood up and nodded, then turned to leave. He stopped at the door and turned. "Nick," he said, "it's OK to love someone, you know. Your wife and kids have been dead a long time."

"No, Rob, no it's not. Not until I know there might be a future for us. Till then, she's just another soldier."

"You keep telling yourself that, brother."

Master Sergeant Agostine knocked on the infirmary door, and heard her say, "Come in." He steeled himself, muttered, "Keep it cool," and opened the door.

Staff Sergeant O'Neill sat up in bed, reading a dog-eared copy of Mark Helprin's "A Soldier of the Great War." Her bandages had been changed, and her face cleaned of blood. Her one clear eye blazed blue, and pierced him again, like her gaze always did.

"Hi Nick," she said, putting the book down. "It's OK, I'm not going to bite you. Yet."

"Let's keep it professional, can we?" he said.

"For now," she answered, patting the bedside.

"Brit, I'm serious."

"Stop having such a stick up your ass, Master Sergeant. The room is too small for you to sit anywhere else."

He did sit down, acutely conscious of how clean she smelled, and how rank he must be. Pulling out a pen and a legal pad, he said, "Give it to me straight, what happened to your team? I know you were on your way to the Highlands, to keep an eye on the Invy Base at West Point."

"We were, and everything was going good. We left here two months ago and..."

Chapter 22

O'Neill tried hard to keep the emotion out of her voice as she lay on the bed, trying to just give a report, but the Master Sergeant could see her struggle. He was drawn down into her story and could picture it in his mind.

The ruins of Newburgh lay spread out in front of them, looking down from the foothills of the Catskills. Team Seven's leader, Chief Warrant Three Alexander, gathered his team around for one last brief before they broke out of the woods and entered Invy controlled territory.

"OK, let's go over this one more time. Nipper, Barton, you're lead pair. Then me and Johnson, followed by Rheam and Burrill, then O'Neill and Chartier. Five hundred meters of separation between pairs, and DON'T let civilians get close to you. Can't violate the three-person rule; you know an orbital or a drone will nail you. Shoot them if you have to to keep them away; we're not losing any people out of kindness."

There were nods and grunts of agreement; this close to the major Invy base at West Point, patrols were sure to be fairly common.

"Route is as follows," he continued, drawing in the dirt with a stick. "52 down to Newburgh, then cut through the ruins of the city, and follow Route 9W. Once we hit the hills, off road through Storm King State Park, till we reach an overwatch point on the West Point Invy garrison. Long weapons will come from the cache in Cornwall at Hudson. IF we get the chance to make the hit, we stand the chance to get instantly hammered. Exfil will be individual or team, RP is Viking if we get split up. Questions?"

Corporal Burrill leaned over and spit out some dip, then said, "Why ain't we coming in from the south, through Harriman or over Bear Mountain?"

Staff Sergeant O'Neill, her red hair hidden up under a NY Yankees ball cap, answered him. "Heavy Invy traffic between the base and the NYC Invy towns. That's why we're going to sneak through the ruins of Newburgh."

"I've been there," chimed in Rheam. He was one of the team snipers, and sometimes he actually took his mind off watching windage and calculating ballistics. "That was a rough town before the war, and I don't think it's gotten any better. No Main Force unit there."

"Nope," agreed Alexander. "Too close to the base. We should be OK, though. Lots of cover."

"We were going to take a shot at a Greenie that was meeting with the Invy to set up another town, Carlyle's his name. He was expected down from Scranton in a caravan; if we could get close enough in there passing over the hill. Rheam was going to try to hit him with a directed radiation beamer, give him a lethal dose to his head."

Agostine shook his head. He hated some of the stuff that R & D came up with and wanted them to try. Yeah, the beam was directional, like a laser, but the Invy sensors could probably pick up any radiation that bounced off hard objects, just like reflected laser light. And you had to hold it on target for almost a second to deliver a high enough dose, which was an eternity in combat. The entire idea was that the radiation would cause cancer, and it wouldn't be traceable to any enemy action.

The walk down from the hills took two days, skirting the water-filled craters that lay across the rail and highway junctions. At one point, they passed the rusting remains of a battery of 105mm howitzers, scattered about like toys, their barrels and trails bent and twisted from the heat of plasma guns, the trucks that towed them burnt to the ground. Close to the ruined guns, the shattered, burned tail rotor of an Apache helicopter still stood mixed with the remains of an Invy Armored Personnel Carrier. As each pair passed the wreckage of the battle, they offered a silent salute to the fallen men and women, but they dared not touch the bones in their rotting uniforms.

"I'm never going to get used to it, Nick. Yeah, there are billions of skeletons around the world, but those were our guys, you know?" He did know, but he let her talk, just squeezed her hand. "I was fifteen, and in JROTC when they hit us, so I wasn't IN, you know, but I was part of it, and I wanted to fight."

"You are fighting," he said, but he knew what she meant. He had been in Pakistan on occupation duty after the Subcontinent Nuke War, and he remembered the mad rush to bring the troops back home, and then the following two years of training to go underground. That year of waiting, after the first strikes, before they ventured back out...

The ambush hit them after Nipper and Barton had passed the silent remains of an office building at dusk, right in the heart of downtown Newburgh. An arrow caught Barton high up in the shoulder, from behind, spinning him around. It was followed by more arrows, and a rush of figures in the dusk, charging at them with a blood curdling howl, ignoring the pistol shots.

If they had all been armed with rifles, or even one belt fed weapon, it would have been over in a minute, but they weren't. The trap closed in as Alexander and Johnson rushed forward, and a separate ambush of screaming savages enveloped Burrill and Rheam

---

"Burrill was done; when you have to shoot to eat, it kind of makes you an expert, and they were using compound bows with razor heads on them. Rheam took cover, and then we came at a run, trying to break the ambush, but there were just too many of them." She closed her eyes, thinking for a minute, then said, "For Christ's sake, they were like a horde of barbarians. They chopped Rheam to pieces, but he went down swinging."

"Brit, they've been growing up in the ruins for ten years. They ARE barbarians."

"I know, but there were ones that were younger than that, throwing pieces of concrete, firing arrows. I shot half a dozen of them. They were KIDS, Nick!" she exclaimed, tears running down her face.

"They wanted your gear and your weapons. You know that. Continue on with your report."

By the time O'Neill and Chartier had closed from the rear, it was almost over. As each pair had come up, they had been hit from all sides by arrows, sling stones, and occasional gunfire. She saw Alexander fall, swarmed by bodies covered in cast-off clothing and rags, carrying clubs.

On the other side of the ambush, Specialist Nipper was carrying his teammate across his shoulders, covered in blood, headed south. Between O'Neill and Nipper stood Johnny Johnson, surrounded by a ring of desperate people, many of them malnourished, with wild, knotted hair. His pistol was in both hands, and even as they closed with him, he fired, knocking down two more, but the rest closed, cutting off his yell of anger abruptly.

"We bailed, Nick. Me and Chartier. The mission was a bust and it was our own people that took us down. We barely made it out; that's when I got hit in the face. Don't know by what."

"You live to fight another day, Brit. What happened to Chartier?" he asked, trying to keep her focused.

She laughed a bitter laugh. "Broke her leg on the way back, greenstick, only a day's walk from here. Stepped into an open manhole that was covered with brush. We went to ground, and I tried to treat her, but hell, SHE was our medic, not me. I'm just a combat lifesaver, with shit for equipment. Blood poisoning set in, and I tried to amputate, but I guess I didn't do a good enough job cauterizing the artery. She bled out while I tried to cut the bone."

O'Neill heard her friend screaming through the belt that was in her mouth, even as she worked feverishly to cut through with the bone saw from the medic kit. She dropped it, her hands slippery with blood, and fumbled around on the floor for the saw, blood from the reopened artery splashing her face, blinding her one good eye. By the time she found the it, the spurts had turned into a dribble, then just a slow leak.

Confused, because there had been a tourniquet on the leg, she wiped her face off and saw that the medic had untwisted it herself, letting the blood flow out. In the end, she knew why. Who would want to live in this damned world with one leg? Or die screaming in agony as the poison raced through her veins?

"We did find Nipper and Barton, on the road outside of town. I don't know how he made it that far carrying Barton, because he had three arrows in his own back. They were both dead."

"Nips was a tough bastard. Well, it's going to happen to all of us, eventually. Anything else to add?"

She sat up on the bed, grabbed his hand, and pulled him closer to her. He started to pull back, but she snaked her other arm around his neck and kissed him hungrily, putting all her grief and loneliness into it. He tried to fight it, but quickly gave up, and kissed her back.

"Brit ..." he said, when they came up for air, "We can't, or more like, I won't. Not till we win. If we do, it's you and me and some brats in a farm house someplace."

"And if we don't?" she asked.

"Then we die together, in battle. I promise."

She looked at him sadly, and said, "I don't want to die, Nick. I want to live and be happy and spend my life with you."

He was helpless in the face of her passion, and when she kissed him again, he surrendered to it.

Chapter 23

CEF Regional HQ, Honshu, Japan

Though the room was deep underground, there was a bit of opulence to the furnishings. Major Takara Ikeda knew that the Empress hated the trappings of state, but it was necessary, in his mind. As both the 'divine' and political head of what remained of the Japanese nation, a little bit of pomp couldn't hurt to remind people of who she was, and, more importantly, what she represented.

So when she entered the room, he took a knee, as did everyone except the two bodyguards that flanked her. Although Empress Kiyomi wore a beautiful blue silk kimono, the two following her carried submachine guns and wore the latest in high tech ballistic armor and communications equipment. They turned and walked out at a word from her; this was her high council, and there was no danger.

"Cut the bullshit," she said, in flawless modern Japanese, and Ikeda hid a small smile. Before being elevated to the throne, Captain Kiyomi Ichijou had been a fighter pilot, and a damn good one, scoring seven kills in the Spratly War, at age twenty-two, flying with the call sign, 'Jiko', or 'Accident'. He knew it was a joke, since nothing she did was by accident.

Around him were gathered the senior members of the Japanese CEF forces, and as he stood, the Major looked around. He feared the bullets of a Power Point slide far more than the ones that came out of a gun, and he had to take a deep breath.

The Empress nodded to Ikeda as she took her seat at the head of the long conference table, and the others sat down after her. He took that as an indication to begin, and he said to the young sergeant sitting behind him, "Please start the presentation."

In the next few minutes, he covered the operation that had resulted in the capture of the Invy Dragon, giving the briefing in dry, clinical tones. The old men who sat around the table kept their faces stonily impassive, except for General Nakura. He alone had argued passionately against the mission, claiming that it would stir up the Invy in reprisal. As the Major talked, Nakura let a more and more unpleasant look creep across his face, a complete breach of protocol.

The other, lower ranking staff officers around him cast their eyes downward, rather than become caught in the staring contest that erupted between the Empress and the General.

Ikeda concluded with, "That is the end of my presentation, but I will answer any questions."

As she opened her mouth, the Empress was cut off by an angry bark from the General. "You had this thing captured, and you just turned it over to the Americans? What if the Invy learn of our role in this? THEY WILL LAY WASTE TO OUR WHOLE NATION AGAIN!" he shouted, slamming his fist down on the table.

The entire room froze, except for the heavily breathing Nakura, and the steely eyed Empress. This confrontation had been coming for quite a while, but usually these things were handled in private. The General must have thought that he had the support of enough of the remaining military to be so bold.

"General Nakura, I appreciate your concern, but I have already heard your reasoning, and I, along with the council, have rejected it."

He seemed to grow even angrier at the dismissal, and shot back angrily, "I do not recognize your authority, CAPTAIN." The disdain in his voice was evident. Ichijou's appointment to the throne, just before the invasion, had been both cheered and protested, with many calling it archaic and unnecessary for Modern Japan. Her assumption of control of the government in the wake of the wholesale destruction of their civilization had caused just as much controversy, but the survivors had been too stunned to do anything but accept her leadership. She had even called for a vote, runners going from Invy town to Invy town, secretly asking if she should continue as head of civilian government, such as it was. Her leadership of the military, as Empress, she did not allow to be questioned.

Now, when they'd had some semblance of peace for nine years, many were loath to rock the boat, as the Americans said. Nakura was the leader of their party, and it had finally come out into the open. Ichijou closed her eyes and sighed, a sad, exasperated exhale.

"I had hoped it wouldn't come to this, General. I looked up to you in the Spratly War, we all did, but this is a different war. Had you called for more aggressive action, I could have forgiven you for insulting my judgement."

"Forgiven me!" he choked out. "You forget yourself, Captain!" he said, refusing to use her honorific of Empress, even though she was, by blood, heir to the throne. "That is to be expected of a woman who does not know her place!"

"General, I will give you one chance to apologize. Then you may go to the surface and commit Seppuku, in the traditional way."

Face bulging outward, the General started to yell at her again, and there was a single CRACK! He sat backward in his seat, a red hole in one side of his head, the aide next to him splattered with bits of blood, brain matter and bone. The Empress hadn't flinched, and Ikeda holstered his own smoking gun.

"Forgive me," he said to her, and knelt, "but I could not allow him to speak to you that way. He was dishonoring our country."

"Oh, get up, Takara. I counted on you, as always. Now, on to Red Dawn. Very appropriate, is it not?"

"Yes, I suppose it is," he answered. Two enlisted soldiers came into the room and removed the General's body. Ichijou told the aide to sit for a while, to think about his former boss. She knew that he also had been an advocate of the 'accommodation' party, and she wanted the lesson to sink in.

"Just so everyone understands," the Empress told the remaining dozen men and women in the room, "Japan will die before we accept slavery. We have waited, and we will strike, and we will burn if necessary. We have been defeated before, and arisen to become a great power, and we will do so again."

She sat back down, kimono rustling, and addressed Ikeda. "Now, Major, tell them what you told me of Red Dawn." Her dark eyes seemed to bore into him, and he felt a stirring in his heart that had disappeared eleven years ago. She was the Empress, yes, but she was a woman, as well.

"On H-hour, to be determined, CEF submarines, gathering off Okinawa, will launch eighty surface to space missiles, armed with nuclear warheads, in an attempt to destroy one of the four orbital stations. Additional submarines will, with laser fire from the North Atlantic, will attempt to blind another. In conjunction with that attempt, CEF forces in North America, Japan and England will attack specified Invy spaceports with the intention of seizing as many assault shuttles as possible, and conducting boarding attacks on the remaining three orbitals, with the intent to seize control or destroy them."

There was dead silence in the room, then the Empress spoke. "In addition to attacking and seizing a shuttle, our contribution to this plan is to provide air cover to the submarines as they launch, since the operation will take at least ten minutes. We will intercept and block Invy fighters from Cam Rahm Bay over the East China Sea, giving the submarines the time they need to complete their end of the mission. Our priority until then is to assemble as many pilots and working planes as we can. Major Ikeda, the scouts will handle getting any fighter qualified personnel as necessary back to their bases. Colonel Shimata," she said to her G4, "yours will be a supreme effort to get those fighters ready. We will be outclassed and out maneuvered, so numbers will count. I expect at least a dozen. Do you understand?"

The man nodded, then thought better of it and smiled, answering with an enthusiastic, "Hai, Empress!"

She stood and walked over to the map of Japan that hung on the wall. "At the same time this is happening, you will strike at the Invy garrison here on Honshu. All Main Force units will start planning for Operation Ryū today. Do I make myself clear?"

They responded with vigor, caught up in her confidence. Major Ikeda, though, had noticed her change in the use of the word "we" to "you" when speaking of the different missions.

"Empress," he spoke hesitantly, "you cannot."

She knew exactly what he was referring to, and arched an eyebrow at him. "I can, Major, and I will. Captain Jiko will be far more useful to Japan in the air, than a closeted Empress Ichijou, hiding underground, will she not?" She smiled at him, a personal, bitter smile, then turned and walked out of the briefing room.

Chapter 24

The road to Raven Rock wound far through the hills of Northern Pennsylvania, climbing up and down hills and making its way through depopulated valleys. This area had been hit hard by the starvation and break down of civilization, and the Invy rule had left little but small homesteads.

They passed other travelers, some walking and some on horses, and spent the hours talking. By the fourth day, they had gone from Colonel and General to Rachel and David, and she had finally come to respect the man. He still grieved over his sister and nephew, but like most of the survivors of this hell world, he had a very hard skin that scabbed over quickly. She knew it was still there, but pushed way down deep. There would be a reckoning someday, she knew. There always was.

"You've been pretty isolated up on your farm," Singh said as their horses grazed in an overgrown state park. "What do you want to know about the state of the world?"

"Everything and nothing," he answered. "I have a pretty good idea of how things stand in Central New York, and a vague idea about the world. We laid pretty low."

"Well, you know about the thirty-degree plague. From what we can tell, the Earth's population stands around five hundred million, probably less. Europe is a shithole, though there is still a functioning CEF Command in Scotland. We had contact with the Swiss two years ago, and they have military forces, but without radio, there's no effective way to coordinate with them. Travel through what's left of France and Germany is too dangerous."

"Dangerous how?" asked Warren, wrinkling his nose at the smell coming from a bad MRE. Meatballs in Marinara Sauce had become Meatballs in Maggot Sauce.

"For some reason, the Invy don't occupy it. They just pound it flat every now and then, so it's reduced to a state of complete barbarism. Target practice, maybe."

He dug around for another MRE, one that was still good. "What about Israel?"

"Gone. They used nukes on the Invy once they started landing, after the two-year pause, and got turned into an extension of the Mediterranean." She poured water into the heater bag and placed it on a rock or something. "The *Alabama* explored the area three years later, landed a Scout Team where Tel Aviv used to be, and nothing."

"The *Alabama*? We still have ships?"

She mumbled something, trying to wash down crackers and cheese. Finally getting it down, she said, "Yes, five American and three Russian. Four bases for them also. Azores, McMurdo, one in eastern Siberia, another, and the last in the South Pacific somewhere. Even I don't know where that one is; Archangel keeps her cards close."

"Who is Archangel?" he asked, sounding merely curious. "I assume you still have some leadership. Who's in charge now? Murphy? Stankowitz? Wait, you said she. Is it that old bat Mercel?"

"I've said too much already," she said bluntly. "You may have me convinced of your role in the defeat, but there are many who will want you shot."

That put a damper on their conversation, and both finished eating in silence. When they had mounted their horses and set out again, Warren probed her for information about the Invy.

"What is there to know? Why do you want to know?" she asked.

""If you know the enemy and know yourself, you need not fear the result of a hundred battles. If you know yourself but not the enemy, for every victory gained you will also suffer a defeat. If you know neither the enemy nor yourself, you will succumb in every battle," he answered.

Her response betrayed her slight annoyance. "Yes, I know, you were very well educated. Lot of good that did you, and us."

"Colonel, I didn't know the enemy, and apparently, I didn't know us, either," he said, then continued, "I thought that I was to be allowed full command, even if it came to a retreat, but I didn't know the politicians that were running things. The Generals I was supposedly in charge of were, at that level, politicians too, and didn't hesitate to stab me in the back when it became expedient."

"They paid for it, though, didn't they?"

A sad, melancholy look grew on his face at the mention. "Yes, yes they did. Cheyenne Mountain fell last, but it did fall, and not to orbital bombardment, either. I was there, in my cell, when the Wolverines hit us. My friends ... they gave their lives to get me out."

They rode on in silence for a bit, starting up a long grade that, a little more than a decade ago, would have been filled with trucks feeding America.

"You know about the towns already," said Singh, after a bit. "Do you know about the slave gangs? Repairing environmental damage, or so they say?"

He nodded. "I've heard of them. Replanting, cleaning up toxically contaminated earth, yadda yadda."

"Well, it's all bullshit. They're mining the remains of our civilization. Gold, platinum, rare earth metals. I think they do it for shits and giggles; there's plenty of that in space. It's just another way to kill off our surplus population."

"You don't believe their propaganda about saving the Earth for the Human race?"

She laughed, an entrancing sound. "Hell no. We aren't sure why they're here, but they have slave races on eleven planets. Not a single race that they've encountered or uplifted has escaped their subjugation, if the records from the scout are correct."

"So why the uplift?" he asked, not knowing much about it.

"Maybe to keep us all at each other's throats. I don't know, and I don't think anyone else does, either. I have to tell you, though, the Cetin and Great Apes have pretty much told them to piss off. The whales actively help us with communications, sending whale song across thousands of miles of ocean and allowing the subs to communicate. I think the dolphins do it for shits and giggles, honestly."

She smiled, then her face turned serious. "You know about the fighting pits, right?"

"No, what are they?"

"The Wolverines and Dragons pit humans against each other as a form of entertainment. That's where Master Sergeant Agostine lost his leg; he kept beating his human opponents, mostly criminals and trash, until he came up against a guy he knew from the service and refused to fight him. The wolverines tied off his leg, chewed it off just below the knee while he watched, and then ate it raw in front of him while the Dragons laughed."

"How did he get out?" asked Warren.

"Someone got word to me. I went in and got him. I don't leave my people, General," she said, with a bit of accusation in her voice.

He ignored her tone and asked about the rules that allowed them to travel with pistols, but no long arms. "You can have them in your house, but not on the road. I never could figure that."

"Easier surveillance for them. They have the orbitals, and around the towns and bases, drones that do pattern recognition. Know how many farmers have gotten smoked for carrying a two by four or a piece of PVC pipe back to their farm after salvaging?"

"Anyway," she continued, "what it comes down to is that, inside the towns the Invy are brainwashing people, especially the kids, into being their slaves, and outside the towns they're slowly killing everyone off. It's time for us to strike back; now or never."

"Strike back how?" he asked, but just then his horse shied at something unseen, and Warren fought to bring the animal under control. When he had, he turned back to see that Singh had her pistol pointed at him, and held a pair of handcuffs in her other hand. On either side of her horse, two extremely serious looking men pointed M-6 carbines at him, looking through combat optics.

"Put these on, David. I'd hate to have to shoot you, though some would give me a medal."

Chapter 25

Russian Naval Base

The Dragon paced back and forth within its cage, arms bound behind it and a blindfold over the reptilian eyes. It was bereft of its gold armor, and instead was clad in a re-sewn navy coverall. Around its neck, though, still hung the translator. Dried out, it seemed to be working fine, translating both threats and curses.

Danielle Morano, PhD in Xeno-biology, and the foremost Invy expert on Earth, watched impassively. To her, the Invy were nothing more than a problem to be solved, or disregarded. To be honest, humans often were too, and she made no bones about being a sociopath. A controlled one, though. She saw no point in hurting those around her, because she could gain nothing from it.

"So how are you going to do this?" asked Captain Larken. She stood a full head taller than the diminutive Morano, but felt very uncomfortable in her presence. Something about her reminded the sub commander more of the alien in front of them than an actual human being. Sure, Morano didn't have six limbs and vertically slanted eyes, but she gave off the same vibe of disinterest.

After getting no answer, she pressed on. "I mean, we don't exactly know much about their psychology. How do you play good cop/bad cop with an alien?"

Morano laughed, a deep, rich sound that surprised the older woman. "You don't," she answered, and turned to a man who had come aboard as soon as they had surfaced in the underground base. He was dressed in the camo of the Russian Federation, but wore a leather apron over his uniform, and a twisted, gnarled beard hung form his face, streaked with white. "Vasily, it's time for us to get to work. Captain, can you send one of your machinist mates up here with a blowtorch? Oh, and you might want to open all your hatches to get the smell out. Charred flesh can be, um, unsettling."

"You're not doing that on my boat, lady!" exclaimed the Captain.

Morano turned from her contemplation of the pacing Invy, and looked at Larken with pale blue, dead eyes. "May I remind you,

Captain, while you may not like it, I have direct authority from Archangel to use whatever tools are necessary, including *you*," she emphasized, "to complete this mission? If I want to take this entire ship out to the middle of the Pacific and sink it as an experiment, with the entire crew aboard, I DAMN WELL WILL!" she almost screamed.

Unseen by the scientist, Chief Ball rested his hand on his belted holster. Larken gave a slight shake of her head, and was about to reply, when they were interrupted. From the cage area, the Invy was hissing in what was, unmistakably, laughter.

Morano instantly shifted her focus away from the Captain, and walked over to the cage, resting her hands on the bars. The Invy hissed at her, laughter gone, and they stared at each other for a full minute. Larken couldn't help but think that she was actually looking at two alien species, both devoid of humanity. Then the xenobiologist snapped her fingers, and the Russian stepped forward. From under his apron he removed a leather bundle, and laid it out on a table, opening it to reveal a gleaming set of surgical tools.

"Barbarians!" hissed the Dragon's translator, and it was Morano's turn to laugh.

"You, who enslave whole worlds and kill billions, call US barbarians? Prepare to feel the pain of an entire world."

Captain Larken motioned for Chief Ball to follow her out of the room. In the corridor, he turned to her and said, "Captain, she's fucking nuts!"

"I know, Bill," she sighed, "but it might be the only way. We need to know the location of the virus labs and stocks, or else everything is going to be for nothing." She winced at the sounds that started issuing from the closed door, a high pitched, keening scream.

It took less than a day. "Like most bullies, they're really cowards at heart," said Dr. Morano as she sat in the base conference room. With her were Captain Larken and Major General Dmitri Levanov, the base commander. The Russian said very little; after the suppressed rebellion a few months ago, he had focused his energy on rehabilitating the base, without much support. The Russian Government in Exile was in the Urals, and could only communicate by foot or horse, a journey across Siberia that took months.

"Just tell us what you learned," said Captain Larken. "Did you find where the virus labs and stocks are located?"

Morano stared at her without blinking until the sailor looked away, uncomfortable. "Of course I found out where they are. That was the whole point."

"Well, then get to the point," rumbled the bear-like Russian. "And don't try to play your little head games with me, you *sumasshedshiy chelovek!*"

The scientist laughed at him, and said something back in Russian, making the officer go pale. Then she laid a report on the table. "The labs are at what was Saigon, or Ho Chi Minh City, as we suspected. The bad news is that the actual viral stocks are contained in the orbitals. There are the 30 degree viruses, and also a general purpose one. They're delivered by orbital drop, command controlled at Saigon."

Larken let out a slow breath that she didn't realize she had been holding, and said, "Shit."

"Is that a problem, Captain?" asked Morano. "Can't you just send some people in to take them out?"

Realizing that the xenobiologist was out of her depth on military operations, she answered simply, "It's not that easy."

"Well, I've done my job, and I'd like to get back to examining the corpse. I need to do a proper autopsy."

"You killed it?" asked the Russian, incredulously.

A look of puzzlement came across the doctor's face. "Of course! I have much to learn about their biology, and it's hard to examine their insides when they are still alive."

Larken and Levanov both palmed their faces, causing Morano to ask what was wrong. "What if, I don't know, we wanted to know WHY they're here on Earth?" spat out the Captain.

"Oh, I asked. I didn't think you wanted to know. It's pretty simple, really." Then she sat still, writing on a legal pad in front of her.

After a full minute, the two military personnel looked at each other, then looked back at her. "Well?" asked Larken, impatience creeping into her voice.

"Well what? I thought we were done," said Morano.

"WHY THE HELL ARE THEY HERE ON EARTH?!" bellowed the Russian.

Morano narrowed her eyes and gave a wickedly evil look at him. "It's in my report, if you want to read it. But if you must know, they really did believe in the environmental stuff when they started, in a way. Their home world is pretty much wrecked, pollution, over population. When they discovered wormhole tech, the first planet they found was the wolverine home world. It was easy to conquer, since the wolverines weren't uplifted yet, and then they got a taste for it. Power corrupts, I guess. They have a fairly feudal political structure, and each Dragon gets to carve out his own estate, so to speak."

"Why Earth though?" asked Larken.

"Just the next one they could reach. I haven't taken time to study the astrophysics involved, though I may do so."

"Did you find out anything about the tactical situation in space? What they have outside the orbitals? Is their fleet still there?" demanded the sub commander, growing exasperated.

"Huh," said the scientist, a puzzled look on her face. "I didn't think to ask."

Chapter 26

Raven Rock, CEF North American HQ

The cell they had him in was bare except for a metal toilet and a wooden bunk bed. Food was brought three times a day, and the lights shut off for what he assumed was eight hours. Other than the Military Police at the far end of the corridor, David Warren saw no one.

He spent the time re-thinking the battle in space, trying to figure out how he could have done anything differently. The only thing he could come up with was to have used the Earth ships as kamikazes, to hopefully smash their way into the Invy ships. Like his instructors had told him though, hope is not a plan. They should have had an alternate plan, but, going off all the technology in the Invy scout, they thought they could win. Even he hadn't thought that a scout was a plain, simple ship, without shields.

It's what that kid in the book would have done, suicide this ships, and he knew that, had he ordered it, they would have. But that was just a book; this was real. There wasn't time, in the middle of the battle, to wrestle with his conscience. Just the argument with his 'superiors' to fall back, disengage, and try to negotiate. It had come as a shock to him that he actually HAD superiors; he had thought that he had been given command of all CEF units. If they had disengaged, they could have had time to run, hide in the asteroid belt, rethink their plans; come up with new weapons and tactics.

The cutting off of his ansible connection, and the four MPs who had wrestled him to the ground and hauled him away, had come only a minute into his argument about retreating. The following week had been spent in a cell similar to this one, deep in the bowels of Cheyenne Mountain. A swift, televised court martial, and then back to the cell, amidst the beginning of the orbital bombardment.

Now he stared at the wall, and thought. Thought about the future. He held no grudge against Rachel Singh; she could just as easily have shot him and brought his head back with her. Likewise, the Scouts had just been doing their job. That their presence had made Jeremy go off and attack an Invy patrol was just the spark that had set him off. It would have been something else.

To pass the time, he dwelled on the bits and pieces of information that he had been told, or overheard. He had passed into Raven Rock blindfolded, but the smell of diesel and jet fuel, and the far-off whine of a turbine engine winding up and down as someone tested it for maintenance, told him much. Likewise the many different voices he had overheard told of a great number of personnel, and he began to hold out some hope. The mention of the submarines meant that they had actual assets, sea and air power, plus ground combat troops.

He was interrupted by a cockroach clambering up the wall of his cell, and he took his boot off and tried to smash it. He hit it square, but the insect bounded away when he lifted the boot. Then it scrambled through the bars, turned and stared at him. In the harsh light of the lamps, he could see it better, and it seemed to have a faint metallic sheen to it.

"You're a goddamned drone, aren't you?" he asked it, knowing he wouldn't get an answer. "Did Singh send you down here to spy on me?" That didn't make sense; it would be too easy to put cameras in the cell.

Down the hall, the door opened, and one of the guards stepped in. The drone/cockroach skittered away down the hall, and Warren watched it go, puzzled. Were there other players in this game that he didn't know about?

Before the guards made it down the hallway, the drone reappeared, followed by more than a dozen others. They climbed the wall opposite his cell, and formed a letter. He watched in astonishment as they continued to spell characters out on the wall, scattering when the guards approached, running back into the darkness. Warren's heart beat like thunder, and the blood rushed in his ears, a roaring sound that threatened to overwhelm him.

"General Warren, Archangel wants to see you," said the senior guard, wearing Master Sergeant's stripes. He had the same pale look as all the others; sunlamps could only do so much after eleven years underground.

They took him, blindfolded again and manacled, to an elevator, and he felt it rise for a very long time. When it stopped, and the door slid open, they guided his steps onto a carpeted floor, moving him forward down a hallway, and into another room. He was placed in a chair, but the blindfold wasn't removed.

"General David Warren, Commander, Consolidated Earth Forces," said the voice of Rachel Singh, "you have been charged under the Universal Code of Military Justice with the following," and she made a simple statement, in a flat voice. "Article 85, Desertion, punishable by death."

He waited for more, but no one said anything for a long while. When they didn't, he said, "Is that it?"

"Isn't it enough?" said an unseen man.

"You forgot 'Calling your Chief names, Wishing to punch his pimply face, and Thinking you Sheriffs look like a lot of Tom-Fools'."

Singh snickered quietly, but the man answered angrily, "What the hell are you talking about? You're about to be shot!"

"It's a quote from a very old book, Colonel Curtis. You should read it sometime. It's about triumphing over darkness when all hope is lost," said a woman, whose voice sounded scratchy and old. There was something hauntingly familiar to it, too, but Warren just couldn't place it. Maybe one of his old instructors?

The prisoner cleared his throat and said, "If any of you were present at the Pentagon, as high ranking officers, you know I got the shaft. We couldn't have won that fight, and I tried to extract what forces I could in the face of a disaster. My orders were countermanded and my ansible connection was cut. You know that, so either shoot me, or not. Please get this over with."

There was a murmured debate that he couldn't hear, and then the woman's voice said, very clearly, "Please leave the room, everyone, except Colonel Singh." With a scraping of chairs and a few murmured "Yes, Ma'am's," then the final closing of a door, the space fell quiet.

"Rachel, do you believe him?" asked the old woman.

After a moment's hesitation that made his heart stand still, she answered, "Yes, Ma'am, I do."

"I agree. Take off his blindfold."

The light blinded him for a moment, and he tried to blink it away, attempting to raise his hands to his face, forgetting he was cuffed. Slowly his eyes adapted, and first he saw Singh sitting at a chair in front of him, her pistol laying on her lap.

Behind the Indian, rolling forward into the light, was a gray-haired woman, face horribly scarred and very thin, in a wheelchair. She had an IV drip running down to her arm, but there was still strength in the muscles that pushed the chair forward, and her sky-blue eyes were clear.

"It's been a very long time, David," she said.

Colonel Singh stood and unlocked his handcuffs as David Warren stared at the woman in front of him.

"B,b,but," he stuttered, a habit he had overcome long ago, "you, you, you're dead!"

"Not yet," she answered, a bitter smile on her burned and withered face. "Soon, but not yet."

Part II

Chapter 27

"Rachel, can you please give us a minute?" asked Warren.

"Of course," she answered, and stepped out of the room.

Kira Arkady, former commander, CEF Fleet Carrier *U.S.S. Lexington,* said nothing, just looked at him. The boy she had loved when they were both teenagers had grown into a man, with some gray in his hair, and hard lines on his face. She liked what she saw, and wished the wish she had made so many times. In a different world...

In turn, he looked at her. Although, like him, she was only twenty-eight, her body looked ravaged, both with the scar tissue on her, and various blotches on her skin that he guessed were cancerous. Her hair was thin and white where it wasn't gray, but beneath the lines was that smile that he had known so well. On the collar of her uniform glittered the five-star insignia of General in Command of Combined Earth Forces, the same insignia he had worn.

"Kira ... I... I didn't know. I would have found you, somehow."

"If I had found you, I would have killed you, David. Right up until a few minutes ago, I still would have. You owe Rachel your life."

He breathed out, then stood up, walked two steps and kneeled in front of her, taking her withered hand in his. "I did hesitate, because I loved you. But I knew, in the back of my mind, that there was no hope. I was trying to plan a way to extricate what was left, to save some strength, when you took that railgun hit. I thought you were gone, your ansible blinked out."

She squeezed his hand with feeble strength, and said, "I hated you for eleven years, Dave. I thought you were a coward; I only knew what people had reported, what we picked up after the lifeboat got us down. Last month one of the teams found Vice Admiral Smithson, living down in Florida. I just got word from them earlier today, which is why I had you brought out of your cell."

"Smithson, the J-2, intel officer?"

She nodded and said, "Yes. He verified everything that happened to you."

"Did you bring him here to testify for me?" Warren hadn't seen anyone else in the cells.

Again the bitter smile. "No, the Team Commander executed him. It's the standing order when we find anyone above the rank of O-6 who was stationed at Cheyenne or the Pentagon."

He started to say something, but realized that, really, he had no answer to that. Instead, he asked her how she had survived.

"Almost the entire crew managed to get off, after our fighters made a desperation run at the Invy battleship that was targeting us. It held off their main gun fire long enough for me to launch lifeboats. And say goodbye to the Lady. Last I saw her, she was going ballistic towards deep space."

He reached up and touched the scars on her face, then kissed her gently. "I have missed you every day, beautiful girl."

Bitter tears ran down her face, and she said, "Not so beautiful now. I ... I'm dying, David. I took a really heavy dose of radiation when we got holed. The docs gave me six months to live more than a year ago."

Anger welled up in him. Anger at the Invy, at the fools who thought that they could win a war on the Invy's turf, and mostly at himself. She saw the look on his face, and understood the emotions he was feeling. She had let her own hatred keep her alive for these long years; hatred of the aliens, hatred of him.

"I let you down, Kira. I let everyone down," he whispered, eyes closed. "I should have tried harder…"

"You're goddamned right you should have, you son of a bitch!" exclaimed a voice from the doorway, and Warren turned to face the man in the doorway, with the voice of the officer he had heard earlier. He stood there with an old M-9 Beretta held on both of them, and behind were several others, all heavily armed.

General Arkady looked at Colonel Curtis, and said to him, in a quiet, steady voice, "You saw the testimony of Vice Admiral Smithson, Mike."

"I did, and it's bullshit. More ass covering for you political officers. People say anything when they're facing the gun. You probably had one of Singh's scouts read him a script, to protect your boyfriend. I'm sure she'll confess to that, eventually." He stepped aside to reveal the Scout Regiment Commander, duct-taped and zip-tied, standing behind him.

Warren felt the implant in his mind immediately calculate the odds of reaching and engaging the man. He didn't need augmentation to know that it would be useless. He may be able to THINK faster, but it didn't do squat for his reflexes.

"So, what now, Colonel? Is this a coup?" asked Kira, gently. "Is this what it's come down to?"

"General, everyone knows the stress you've been under, planning Red Dawn, and how sick you are. You need to step aside and let someone else handle this."

"I am," she answered. "General Warren will be taking over for me."

"No," retorted Curtis, "he's going to be tried and shot."

"By whom? You? I doubt General McCauley will be OK with that."

At the mention of the Raven Rock base commander, Curtis sneered. "She wasn't."

"Since you're standing here, I assume she's dead."

He didn't answer, just motioned with the pistol, starting to wave the three men behind him forward. With a shock, Warren saw that they all wore green armbands, including Curtis.

"You know the Greens aren't organized," said the Colonel, "and don't even know we're still around. It was quite a shock to Drummond here to find out that the CEF existed. There's a man, one of the Greens, who suspected, and he's been trying to create an organization of people who will work with the Invy, help restore the planet. Drummond was sent to find out whatever he could about us. It was pure luck that that dipshit Agostine admitted the kid to his team."

"Not pure luck, really," said Arkady. "We've been tracking Carlyle for a long time." What she said, though, didn't seem to register with Curtis, who was full of adrenaline from the success of his plan.

Warren felt all the blood leave his head, and the world swam around him. "D-d-d-d-d... DO THE INVY KNOW?" he managed to blurt out.

"No, not yet. There's only a loose network of Greens, and the one man who suspects. He isn't going to go to them until he has proof."

"Why? Why are you doing this?" asked Arkady, simply.

"Because I'm going to work out a treaty with the Invy. And your plan isn't going to work, except to get us all killed."

"Listen, Colonel," said Warren, "you CAN'T negotiate with the Invy. If you do this, there is NO hope, do you understand me?"

He turned to the young man standing next to Curtis. "Drummond, you have been outside. You know what I'm saying is true!"

"General, what I know is that the Invy are here to fix what the old civilization screwed up. It's going to take sacrifice, and generations of work, but from what I've heard of Red Dawn, you're going to screw everything up again. Colonel Curtis and Mister Carlyle will come to an accommodation, and the Invy will listen to us."

"Enough of this bullshit. Warren, come along quietly, so I can shoot you out of sight of your friends. Let Kira live out the rest of her time in peace," said Curtis. Two of the men, both wearing Major rank, stepped forward towards him.

Chapter 28

Two shots rang out, muzzle flashes sparking from the back of the room, and the Majors sprawled on the floor bonelessly, neat entrance holes in their faces, and craters in the back of their heads. Curtis stood, stunned, covered in bone and blood fragments.

"Thank you, Master Sergeant Agostine," said General Arkady.

"Anytime, Ma'am," came the disembodied voice from the far side of the room.

"Please disarm Colonel Curtis, please, Sergeant Jones. Drummond, drop the weapon."

There was a grunt from Curtis, and his arm, with the pistol in it, was twisted downward, and everyone could hear the bones crushing in his hand. He tried to stifle a grunt of pain, and fought it for a second, but a decade of living underground and working on staff was no match for the seasoned Scout. The pistol started to fall, but another invisible hand caught it.

Drummond stood there, completely undecided. When he had been growing up in Scranton, he used to regularly sneak into the Invy town and, hungry for education, listen to their lectures. Getting as high as he could into the CEF had been his own plan, once he knew they existed, and he had been out of touch with Carlyle since he joined his Main Force unit. The idea of an alliance with the Green leader had just come to him earlier that day, when he saw how bitter Curtis was. He had planned just to take information back to Scranton, tell the Greens all about the CEF, but a casual reference and a conversation with Sergeant Bassily in Operations had led to Curtis approaching him that morning.

Now, in front of him stood the CEF leadership, and he remembered what Carlyle had said when he started his infiltration. "If not, then strike when the opportunity arises." Drummond knew he was dead anyway, so he raised his pistol to shoot. Two bullets struck him almost in unison, punching his body against the wall. He struggled to draw breath for a moment, wheezing, then slumped over sideways, eyes still open but still.

Hoods were removed to reveal Agostine, Jones and Reynolds, disembodied heads floating eerily in the cool air. One at a time, they striped off the rest of the camo, and stepped into the light. Jones was last; he spent some time hog-tying Curtis and then freed Singh.

"You took your time, Nick," said his commander.

"That," answered Arkady, "was my call. We could not move against them until they openly revealed themselves. I regret General McCauley's death, but I assume Captain Padilla is taking care of the rest of them?"

Singh nodded, then motioned to Curtis. "What do you want to do with him?"

Arkady stayed silent for a moment, then said, "Rachel, please help me," tugging at her collar. The scout leader came over and helped her take off the five-star rank.

"Dave, I think these are yours," she said, handing them to the stunned Warren.

He stared at the glittering rank as they lay in his hand, then clenched his fist on them so hard that his knuckles turned white and the pins punctured his skin. Blood started to drip on the immaculate white tile floor, splattering drops of vermillion red to match the cooling corpses. Then he opened his hand and let them drop.

"No."

His refusal echoed around the chamber. Arkady looked shocked; Singh's face held no expression, nor did any of the other scouts.

"I knew it!" sneered Curtis from where he stood, hands cuffed behind him, "A goddamned coward!"

Master Sergeant Agostine shot him in the head, and the body sagged in Jones's grip.

"Damn, Nick. It's gettin like Chicago up in here!" he said, dropping the corpse. He brushed at the splatter on his camo, cursing under his breath.

"Can we move this someplace else?" asked Singh, and took Warren by the arm. "Come with me, Sir."

"Don't call me that," he answered back, but allowed himself to be herded out of the room, pushing Arkady's wheelchair.

That left Agostine, Jones and Reynolds standing with the dead. "I guess it's just enlisted doing the dirty work."

"Can I get a cleanup on aisle five?" said Jones.

Reynolds laughed, but Agostine turned away, looking down at the dead bodies. No laugh, not even a smile. His face set in a grim rictus, and he put his weapon on safe, walking out of the room. "What a fucking waste," he said, looking at Drummond's lifeless eyes, and kicked hard at Curtis' body as he passed.

"Whoops!" said Jones, and he bent down to grab Drummond by the ankles. The teen had a surprised look on his face, and as Jones pulled, the body left a streak of blood across the floor. He dragged the remains over to the other dead men, even as Reynolds pulled one of the Majors over too.

"What the hell was that about?" she asked.

"Nick's been at this since way before the war. He did two tours in Syria, fought in the Spratly War, was a POW in China, all before he was twenty-five. Then the Invy came, and shit, dude's pushing forty now. He's been at this scoutin' stuff for almost two decades, and I guess it's gettin to him, you know? Plus he's all wrapped up in Brit, and his head ain't in the game."

"Damn," she said, grunting as she tried to pull Curtis over. He had been a big man, and his bowels had let go when he died, making the place smell even worse than the coppery tang of blood. Jones came over and helped her, and they piled all four bodies in the center of the room. At the door, two privates showed, manhandling a cart. Another followed, pushing a mop bucket and wiping up the tracks the wheelchair had made through the blood.

"Have at it, suckers!" said Jones. "Be all you can be and all that shit! We gotta go back out to the glorious sunshine, get outta this bat cave." He and Reynolds walked out past the younger soldiers, giving them each a salute.

"Man, they get to shoot the shit out of these officers, and we gotta clean up after them," said one private.

"Yeah, but we can take a hot shower whenever we want. Remember being out in the ruins?"

"Amen to that, brother. And regular food, too."

The grass is always greener.

Chapter 28

"Someplace else" turned out to be a command and control center, down two levels. There were numerous officers who rose to their feet and stood at attention when Arkady was wheeled into the room. Foremost among them was Captain Padilla, who had a splash of blood across the front of his uniform.

"Ma'am," he said, stepping forward. "You took a very big chance letting that kid get close to you."

"War is chance, Jesse," she answered. "All the best laid plans of mice and men go out the window, but we do what we can. It worked out well, though I didn't think they would go after General McCauley first."

She rolled forward, and Warren was conscious of all the eyes on him. Assembled in front of them was, he assumed, the Command Staff of the Combined Earth Forces. Some faces he knew, but he was shocked at how old they had grown. His implant sometimes listed the bio, a decade out of date, of certain people as he glanced at them, but he ignored it.

With a feeble wave of her hand, Arkady motioned for him to stop pushing the chair, and they came to rest at the center of the room. Singh stepped away, leaving the two facing the several dozen people. "At ease, everyone," said Arkady.

"Kira, I don't want this!" Warren muttered to her.

She looked over her shoulder at him, and in her smile, he saw the ghost of the girl he girl he once loved, who was made of harder steel than he was. "I don't care what you want, Dave. It's what you're going to do."

Turning back to the staff, she motioned again, and various screens and monitors lit up, showing views from all around the interior of the giant base. In each, there was gathered a crowd of people, wearing various uniforms, looking back expectantly.

"CEF soldiers," began Arkady in a wavery voice, but then she stopped. When she continued, strength had come back to her, but Warren wondered what the effort was costing her.

"CEF soldiers," she said again, "less than half an hour ago, there was an attempted coup here, by the J-3, Colonel Curtis. He, along with a dozen other plotters, are now dead. I'm sorry to say that, during the attempt, Brigadier General Katherine McCauley lost her life. I was informed of the plot by Lieutenant General Dalpe, the Main Forces Commander, who stayed loyal to us when approached."

She waited a moment, then continued onward. "I want you all to know, publicly, that General Warren, who you all know from the Battle of the Belt, has been found, and is now with us again. What you don't know, and what will not be tolerated ever again, was that Warren was betrayed at a crucial moment of the battle by the very politicians and senior leadership that we had all put our faith in. When it was obvious we were overmatched in technology, Warren attempted to order a retreat to save the fleet, but he was overruled. I know that now, and you all know I should have more reason to hate him than anyone, but I don't. With him in command, he will lead us to a final victory over the Invy." Even as she finished, her voice trailed off in exhaustion, but it was drowned out by the storm of applause and cheers that echoed through the C2 section, and from the speakers.

"No, I will NOT do this!" he tried to protest, but the shouts and cheers drowned him out. David Warren turned and fled, leaving a bloody streak on the doorway where the rank had punctured his hand. Rachel Singh caught up with him at the end of the hallway, and stood in front of him. Warren was breathing heavily, repeating the word "No" under his breath, over and over.

"You," she said angrily, "are going to go BACK in there, and use your goddamned talent, and whatever else you have, to execute Red Dawn and make sure it happens correctly. Do you understand?"

"I …. I can't! It's just like when the fleet sortied, everyone cheering … and they all died."

She slapped him hard across the face, once, and then again. He raised his fist to her in shock, and struck out blindly. Singh easily avoided it and used his momentum to lever his arm behind his back and slam him up against the wall.

"You are going to go back in there," she hissed in his ear, "and LEAD. Or else we are ALL dead. Do you hear me? If you EVER loved that woman, and you are even HALF the man she thinks you are, you will go back in there and give her hope before she dies! For the last ten years, she has given us EVERYTHING she had, and held us together!" Then she let him go and stepped back.

Warren said nothing for a long moment, slumped against the wall, but then slowly straightened. He said nothing to Singh, in fact ignored her, and started back to the command center.

Stepping inside, he said in a loud voice, "I'm sorry, everyone. It was all … a bit much for me. I've been away for a long while. I want a conference in one hour, with full details on Red Dawn." Then, bending over, he held Kira Arkady's hand, feeling the paper-thin skin and wasted muscles.

"Kira," he whispered to her, "let's win." Then he looked Colonel Singh straight in the eye, and smiled.

The conference room was paneled in fake wood, and the inevitable PowerPoint slides were waiting on the end of the table.

"First thing, turn that shit off," said Warren. He was now wearing a full set of CEF camo, with the five-star insignia subdued at his collar. The young Captain who had been about to start the slide show hurriedly gave the voice command, and the screen flickered off.

Warren had spent most of the last hour ported into the base semi-AI, getting a complete download of the current CEF forces disposition and personnel, as well as updates on Invy tech. As he flicked through the information in his mind, he was amazed at how unaware of things he had actually been while he was supposedly "in command."

Operation Moria had been, he learned, one of the most massive undertakings in world history, and it still hadn't been enough. Underground bases had been constructed for ground, air and naval forces, in strategic locations, and stocked with enough supplies to last more than two decades. Ansible connections, those rare and incredibly expensive quantum communicators, had been located at each of the major defense commands, all tied into the network at Cheyenne Mountain. Personnel had been sequestered even before the fighting began.

Warren had known nothing of this; all expenditures, he had thought, had gone to the fleet of sub-light battleships and carriers that had been built at ruinous expense at the L5 point between Earth and the Moon. Apparently not, he mused. This must have cost trillions of dollars.

He thought hard, and a map of the still active bases appeared to hover in front of him. Less than a dozen, not counting the Navy bases that he had already heard about. Raven Rock was the largest in North America, and there was only one other functional base on the continent, high in the Canadian Rockies. Between the two, there was a full division of armored vehicles, many retrofitted with upgrades developed from the captured Invy scout technology. In addition, there were the remnants of a full air group of F-15s, F-16s, F-22s, and even some old A-10s. Raven Rock held more than thirty, but how many would fly, no one knew.

Most of the surviving installations were in the same situation, or even worse. Only three, Raven Rock, Vilyuchinsk, and Tierra del Fuego still had ansible connections, and the South American base was strategically useless. Messages were relayed through the whales or via torturous trips overland.

The problem, he immediately saw, was personnel. There was less than ten percent of the men and women needed to operate the planes, and most were maintenance, caretakers for the pilots who had been lost trying to battle the Invy forces in the initial ground invasion. The armored vehicle situation was both worse, and better. Few base personnel were actual tankers or infantry; but the Main Force units regularly studied how to operate them. In a pinch, they could be called on to crew them. The other problem, though, was that the armor was hundreds of miles away from the largest concentrations of the Invy, and few had been refitted for fusion power. Most still ran on almost non-existent petroleum products.

"None of this matters if we don't take the high ground," he said out loud.

Lt. General Dalpe, an incredibly fit man in his late fifties, nodded. "You see the problem. We probably have enough strength, between the bases and the Main Force units, to wage a pretty effective campaign against Invy ground forces. The problem is, as always, who holds the high ground, and right now, that's the orbitals."

"And whatever of their fleet is still in orbit," added Warren. "Do we have any idea? Didn't we take a prisoner recently?"

Uncomfortable glances were exchanged, until finally a civilian spoke up. His name and position floated in the air over his head, in Warren's vision. Doctor David Johnstone, PhD in particle physics, class of '23 from MIT. His crisp British accent overlaid the hesitancy in his voice.

"We, uh, we did, Sir. But evidently no one told our interrogator to ask such a question. Apparently the Dragon in custody passed away before that could be rectified."

"What idiot forgets to ask a question like that?" exploded Dalpe.

"Apparently my colleague Doctor Morano. I'd hardly call her an idiot, General. Actually, I'd be careful of calling her an idiot. To her face, anyway."

"What's done is done," said Warren. "I want a complete brief on this plan by each of the service heads, and then we're going to sharp shoot the shit out of it. Then I'm going to see how General Arkady is doing."

In the back of the conference room, unnoticed as opposed to unseen, Master Sergeant Agostine leaned over and whispered to Colonel Singh, "Is that the same guy who had a spine like jelly a few weeks ago?"

"His spine wasn't jelly, Nick. He just lost his heart, and now he's found it again. It's amazing what a man will do to prove himself to someone he loves."

Chapter 30

The meeting continued far into the night, with a review of forces, individual plans of attack, and hashing out details. In the bleary hours of pre-dawn, Warren called an end to the brainstorming and asked the new J-3, Lt. Colonel Marsh, to back brief a summary of the plan.

"Sir, at H minus 00:10, the combined submarine fleet will launch interceptor and laser attack on Invy Stations One and Four, with the intent to destroy them or neutralize their offensive capabilities. Their launch point is here, approximately five hundred miles southeast of Japan, and here, three hundred miles off the coast of North Carolina."

Warren interrupted the Colonel with a raised hand, and turned to an Air Force officer seated at the other end of the table. "Major Hollister, can you explain the why behind this?"

"I could, Sir, but it might make some of these knuckle draggers heads explode," she answered, and there was a tired chuckle around the table. She stood and brought up a diagram on the holo, showing Earth with four equidistant points in rotation around it.

"Basically, each station acts as the eyes of the one following it, once it gets past a certain point. In essence, it's difficult to fire a rod backwards from orbit, since they aren't geostationary."

"She said rod," muttered Jones at the back of the room.

"Why are you here again?" whispered Reynolds, elbowing him hard in the stomach. The Scouts had been assigned as bodyguards to Warren, and annoyingly followed him almost everywhere over the last day.

"So if a station has passed over where we are attacking, they pass the actual retaliatory mission back to the next approaching station. One passes over a particular point in the Northern Hemisphere every twenty-two minutes. By blinding Station Four, and nuking the shit out of Station One, we hope to give you roughly forty minutes to complete your objectives."

"Thank you, Captain, for breaking it down. Commander Yu?" he said, turning to the Naval Liaison officer.

"Once at Yankee Station, at the given time, five American submarines will fire off their entire compliment of Surface to Space missiles, armed with proximity burst nukes and bomb pumped x-ray lasers. The remaining US sub will be launching cruise missiles with tactical nukes at the Invy viral labs located at the former Saigon. The two Russian submarines will be off the Eastern seaboard of the US, hitting Station Four with high capacity lasers to damage antenna, optics, and any other surveillance equipment we can."

"Why don't they just use the lasers to shoot down the station?" asked General Dalpe.

Commander Yu answered instantly. "There just isn't enough juice on the subs to power a laser that big, and an unstable platform, atmospheric diffusion, velocity of the station, other things all add up to make it extremely difficult to even hit the target."

"Plus they have maybe ten minutes to attack before the Invy scramble fighters out of Miami," said Captain Hollister. "We're going to provide air cover, but without tankers, it will be at extreme range, and we only have eleven birds here that can get off the ground. Four F-22s, five F-16s, and two F-15s. Every single F-35 is grounded because of code bugs. Can't even start the damn things. The Invy have a dozen of their trans-atmospheric fighters stationed there. They're probably complacent from having no targets for almost ten years, but as soon as the first laser hits, sure as shit those Dragon pilots and their Octos are going to be zipping across the runway."

"Better and better," muttered Warren.

"I can help with that," said Singh. "Scout Team Five will be able to cover that runway with sniper teams. We should be able to get two or three before the base defenses hit back."

Everyone in the room fell silent, realizing that Colonel Singh had just signed a death warrant for one of her teams.

"Listen to me, everyone," said Warren, the hard tone in his voice that had been developing over the past day growing even harder. "People are going to die. Most of us are going to die doing this, but, from what I've seen, it's our only chance. Our hardware is getting old. We're getting old!" he said, hammering his hand down on the table for emphasis.

"I've lived out there," he continued. "I watched a neighbor's baby get eaten alive by Wolverines because they violated a stupid law. My nephew," and he paused for a second, "my nephew attacked an Invy patrol with just one friend and some shitty ass rifles, and lost his life doing so. Jeremy was a better man than I, and braver than any of us."

He looked each of the officers and senior NCOs in the eye, going around the room. "Make no mistake, ladies and gentlemen, this is IT. We either do this now, or we're done for as a free people, and probably as a species altogether. Do you understand?"

Warren didn't wait for their answer, just turned to the Main Force commander and said, "Bob, continue with the ground attack plan."

General Dalpe stood up, and launched into his plan. "Prior to H hour, all Main Force units will infiltrate to within five miles of their objectives, which are the Main Invy regional bases in North America." He brought up a map on the holo, and showed the locations. There were more than a dozen, spaced evenly around the country.

"Each base contains several hundred Wolverines, Armored Personnel Carriers in Company Strength, and a combined Air Intercept/Ground Attack Squadron. We expect to be able to commit, on average, five hundred troops per base, but it's a sucker punch, really. They're going to hit, and then withdraw as soon as the remaining orbital broaches the horizon. The main objective is actually here," and a point on the map lit up, outside where Washington, DC had been located.

"It's closest to Raven Rock, and has a squadron of heavy lift transports that are used to shuttle personnel between ground and the Orbital Stations. Our intention is to seize these shuttles and use them to attack and board the remaining three orbitals, to gain the high ground. Colonel Singh's people will be leading that attack, with an infiltration the night before. The same will be happening in Scotland and Russia."

"Oh shit!' exclaimed Jones loudly, and Reynolds groaned.

"Sir," said Singh to Warren, "please excuse my soldier's enthusiasm for the mission," all the whole shooting Jones a dirty look. In response, he activated his camo and disappeared into the background.

Warren actually laughed, and said, "I understand his reaction, Colonel, because all of us are going to be in on this attack. If it fails, every one of our bases is going to be pounded into dust."

Chapter 31

David Warren returned to his quarters after stopping by the infirmary to see Kira. The discussion they had had couldn't be called an argument; she was too weak for that.

"Kira, this plan, it's insane. It's never going to work. Every single missile is going to get shot down before it hits that station."

"I know," she answered quietly. Whereas the day before she had seemed a tower of strength, twenty-four hours later, the General seemed a withered shell of her former self. His implant gave him access to her vitals through the base wireless, and although he wasn't a doctor, even he could see the red flashing numbers that hovered over her.

"David, I know the plan sucks, but it's all we have left. I have faith in you that you can do this. You always were the best, you know."

"I was then. I don't know about now. One thing that bothers me, Kira, is this. What happens AFTER? How the hell are we going to rebuild our civilization? What happens when they come back, even if we kick them off Earth?"

She smiled gently, making his heart beat faster, and said, "That won't matter to me, will it?"

"How can I do this without you?" he asked her, squeezing her hand harder than he intended to. Unbidden tears rolled silently down his face.

She ignored the pressure, and squeezed back. "You have good, competent people around you, Dave. Especially Colonel Singh, and I think she likes you more than she lets on. We women know these things. Still," she sighed, her breath a harsh whisper in her throat, "it was good to see you again, before I went."

"I've always loved you, Beautiful Girl. There was never anyone else," he whispered.

She smiled, and said, "Idiot. Of course there wasn't."

With that, she had slipped back into sleep, her hand falling out of his. A stern-faced nurse came in and pushed him out of the room with a barked command, his rank notwithstanding.

Warren himself was exhausted after the all-night planning session, but now, in his room, he couldn't sleep. The events of the last month swam before him, and the responsibility he bore weighed down on him again. He didn't see how what they were doing was anything but a very long shot. Red Dawn was set to happen by the end of October, in three months, which was bad timing in his opinion. Better to attack when it was hot out, to confuse scanners and make the Wolverines less effective. He couldn't change the date, though. Too much had already gone into planning.

The other thing nagging him was the drone insects he had seen. He knew that they wouldn't approach his quarters; a scrambler field, designed to prevent, well, bugs, would fry any limited AI they would have. Down by the prison cells was a different matter, but here, no. There was really only one thing for him to do.

He gently opened the door and called for PFC Reynolds, who was standing guard outside his door. "Tiffany, can you do me a favor? Colonel Marsh has some hardcopy files I want to review. Please go down to the Ops Center and get them, will you? I'll be asleep when you get back, so just slip them under the door."

The scout eyed him shrewdly, but Warren just looked back at her with some impatience. "Now, PFC," he said, emphasizing her rank. He had come a very long way from the man who sat paralyzed as his home was destroyed. She nodded and walked off down the corridor. Though tempted to watch her get in the elevator, he shut the door and quickly started packing.

Taking off the uniform, he dragged a bundle of his civilian clothes out from a locker under the bed, exchanging all but the boots. Placing his 10mm issued sidearm on his belt, he pulled on a hoodie, covering the pistol. While he dressed, he called up schematics of the facility in his implant, looking for the best way out.

The most likely exit to be unguarded was the fusion reactor cooling water export. The pipe ran through a tunnel for a mile underground to cool it before being discharged back into the river, to avoid detection. Alongside it ran a service access tunnel, and he could see through his implant that there were no personnel anywhere near it. It had probably been ten years or more since the tunnel access was opened to the outside.

Opening the door, he saw no one in the corridor, and he slipped out towards the stairs at the opposite end from the elevator. He figured that he had maybe eight hours head start, plenty of time to get off the facility.

The first bump in his plans came as he descended the stairway, flight after flight. On the ninth landing, he almost collided with a Sergeant coming up the stairs. The young woman gaped at him for a second, star struck, and it allowed him a split second to think.

"Um, excuse me, Sergeant. Where is the Officers' Mess?" he asked.

"Two more floors down, Sir," she answered, recognizing him despite his civvies, standing at rigid attention, eyes locked forward. One good thing, he had noted, was that the surviving CEF enforced rigid discipline. Another good thing was the way her chest stood out while at attention … Snap out of it, he yelled at himself.

"Thank you, Sergeant," he answered, and walked on past her.

The rest was easy. After the initial fighting, Warren had spent months travelling across the devastated land, hiding by day and moving at night, with the goal of getting back to his sister and her family. Slipping through the machinery of the fusion plant and finding the access door was relatively simple, and his interface with base net opened the locked door easily.

Walking down the mile-long corridor, he thought about how it would look, but there was no helping it. This had to be done, the letters formed on the wall by the drones left him no choice. If there were any chance that Red Dawn was to succeed, he had to do it, and what he hoped might be possible seemed like an even slimmer chance.

The exit had a simple mirror arrangement, allowing the person on the inside to see if there was any threat outside. The entrance was camouflaged to look like part of the rock wall of a secondary road cut, and blended in perfectly.

Seeing nothing after waiting for more than half an hour, he said to himself, "Goodbye, Kira," and worked the locking mechanism, stepping out into the morning sunlight. Outside, it was a warm August day. He made his way through the pine forests, climbing steadily upwards towards the summit of a ridge, always aiming in a westward direction.

Sergeant Sasha Zivcovic watched him through the scope of his sniper rifle, ignoring the pain of his still healing wounds. "Should I take the cowardly son of a bitch out now?" he asked Doc Hamilton. His finger rested lightly on the trigger, but the Senior NCO knew that Ziv wouldn't fire on THIS target without his say so.

"Nope, you know Nick's orders. Follow him, and see what he's up to. I don't think he's running away from something, I think he's running *toward* something. Boyd, get your ass back to the Raven Rock exterior guards, send word for the rest of the team."

The younger man said nothing, just nodded and took off running eastward, towards the nearest hidden guard post.

Chapter 32

Western Kansas, six weeks later.

The town looked deserted, but David Warren knew that could very easily be a lie. He had almost gotten into a bad jam east of the Mississippi twice, looking for food. The horse he rode was a valuable commodity, and there was still a healing gunshot score on its flank

Getting across the rivers had been hard, and he had only managed to cross the Mississippi by paying a boatman with five precious 10mm cartridges. Only four we left; the rest had been expended in a brutal gunfight north of St. Louis that left him shaking, and two men dead. There had been one CEF cache along his route, in Western Missouri, but when he got there, there was nothing left but broken boxes and MRE wrappers. Since then, he had been riding hard across the Kansas plains, occasionally swapping out horses with known sympathizers along the way. The last of those had been two hundred miles ago, though, and both he and the horse were worn out. His water was about gone, too.

Ahead lay the Kansas/Colorado border, and there was a barricade thrown up across the road, a battered school bus. Around them stretched hundreds of miles of empty plain, gently rising, and what was left of the ruined town, a mile behind the barrier. Food was running low; not for the horse, but for him, and he would hate to have to shoot the animal just to eat it. They could go far around, swing south twenty miles, and avoid it, but he needed supplies. If the town were empty, he could probably scavenge something. If it wasn't, well, there was the bow on his back and the two remaining pistol rounds. Either fight or trade. He didn't like the look of things, though. Scattered here and there in the grass were jumbles of bleached bones.

The decision was made for him when two horsemen rode out from around the bus. They carried stubby MP-5s, and rode easily, clad in bits of old CEF uniforms. Both had long beards, but looked fairly well fed. There was probably at least one more behind the bus; no one wanted to violate the rule of three and get nailed by an orbital. Out here you could risk it, as the nearest Invy town was a hundred miles south, but smart people didn't.

"Sergeant," said Warren, as the men road up, meaning the older of the two. The stripes of his rank were still loosely attached to the tattered uniform collar.

"Traveler," answered the man in acknowledgement, but there was no politeness in his tone. "Let's see what you've got, starting with that pistol. Take it out, real slow, left hand, butt first."

Warren cursed inwardly. To have made it this far... some tactical genius he was. The isolation of the plains and the friendly reception at the last homestead had made him drop his guard. Better to give them what they wanted, and try to talk his way out of it.

"Think maybe you guys have some food? I've got some Invy credits."

"Ain't no Dragon shit good round here, with the CEF in charge," said the other one, a sallow faced teenager. His only concession to military rank was a patrol cap squashed down on his head, but the submachinegun was well maintained and pointed directly at Warren's chest.

Fifteen hundred meters away, Reynolds and Zivcovic lay underneath the grass colored blanket that they had thrown over themselves to prevent being silhouetted on the small hill. The redhead watched the bus with her spotter scope, looking for the potential third person. Behind them and slightly lower, Singh flashed a mirror southwards, signaling to the flanking team of Hamilton and Boyd. The northern flankers, Agostine and O'Neill, would get the same signal, if she could get the sun to angle correctly.

"There he is," said Reynolds. "Caught a flash off his scope. Farther back than I expected, corner of the leftmost building, that charging station. Behind the wrecked tow truck."

"That is ... almost two thousand meters," said her partner as he eyed the wind patterns in the tall grass.

"Can you make it?" she asked as he repositioned his rifle to find the target. He just spit on the ground in answer, nestling his Sako TRG-42 closer into his shoulder. Arrogant prick, she thought. See if he gets any from me tonight.

They waited to see what would happen, since their orders were to fire only if it looked like Warren was in serious trouble. Only twice before, once when he had been in that fight north of St, Louis, had the team acted. In that case, an unseen third man who had tried to stab the General in the back caught a round in the head, and fell back into the kinetic crater that the three attackers had come from.

The second time had been when, after they established the direction he was heading in, the lead team had come across two cannibals, roasting the leg of a child in the ruins of a medium sized town. That fight had been short and brutal, Hamilton and Boyd showing no pity for them.

They had been lucky, too, in that Invy patrols had taken their usual summer hiatus. The Wolverines hated moving around when the temperature was over ninety, and the CEF took full advantage of that. Still, being out in the middle of nowhere helped, too. No drones, just the orbitals watching, as always.

Now, as Singh slid under the blanket with them, the Colonel debated what to do. Warren was heading somewhere, and she thought she had an idea where, but for what? Every time she had considered catching up with him, something had made her hold the team back.

Before she could open her mouth, there were a series of pops, pistol fire, one shot, two quick, a ragged burst of submachine gun fire, and then one more. She felt more than heard Ziv fire just after the first pop, then again before the fourth one. She whipped her binos out and focused in on Warren, who was still on his horse, but slumped down. One horse was down, and a third shot from Ziv hurtled its rider back as he tried to struggle out from under. The other horse ran, riderless, towards the west.

"Shit!" exclaimed Singh, and started to scramble out from under the blanket. "COVER ME!" she yelled, and vaulted onto her horse, whipping it into a gallop. She felt another round from the sniper crack past her, even as three more horsemen appeared from around a building. Rifle fire cracked from the small town, kicking up dust around her. What the hell had they stumbled into?

She cursed herself for not contacting Warren earlier, and dodged her horse to one side to give Ziv a clear shot, drawing her own pistol and riding straight at the riders, down to two now. When she was twenty meters from Warren, she fired, no chance of hitting, but hoping to throw off their aim.

A thud against her chest, and she grunted as the closer one let off a wild burst from his machine pistol, blood splattering from her horse's head and another round slamming into her body armor, even as one of her wild rounds caught the shooter in the side of his face. Horse and rider fell in a tumble, and Singh rolled free. Scrambling for the pistol, she grabbed it and started firing in the general direction of her attackers. Warren lay ten meters from her, holding his own shoulder and crawling toward one of the dead men. The last man was reloading on the gallop, swapping magazines, when his head erupted and he tumbled backwards out of the saddle, a hundred meters away.

Singh ran over to Warren and dragged him behind the dead horse, and quickly started checking his wounds. A 9mm submachine round had plowed through the meat of his shoulder, and it was a mess. He screamed in pain as she put her gloved hand on it, squeezing it shut as she frantically tore open a pressure bandage with her teeth. With her free hand, she slapped it on the wound, and then placed his own hand over it.

"Hold this in place," she grunted as she wound the cloth strips tight around the bandage. Then she risked a glimpse over the top of the horse.

There were three dead men, no, four. One was still alive, a woman, gut shot and making feeble crawling motions in the direction of the wrecked bus. Singh retrieved one of the MP-5s, checked the chamber, and fired a shot into the woman's skull. She flopped once and then lay still. The rifle fire had dwindled off to a few lingering shots, and then stopped all together. They weren't going to waste ammo when they were hopelessly outclassed; probably withdrawing even now.

"About time you showed yourself," hissed Warren through his pain. "I, I, k,knew you were back there ever since I got t,t,to Kansas," he stuttered. "Just didn't know w,w,who…"

Singh laughed, adrenalin still coursing through her, joyous at their survival, though her ribs hurt. "We must be losing our touch!"

Chapter 33

It was night before they could move away from the dead horses. Warren's bleeding had stopped, and she had injected nanos into the wound. He was higher than a kite, and moved along complacently.

They met Reynolds and Zivcovic halfway back to the small hill, and the other two scouts quickly erected an IR proof tent over them, while staying outside on guard. An hour later, Sergeant O'Neill crawled into the tent and kicked Singh out after getting an update on Warren's condition.

"He's comfortable now, and Doc Hamilton will take that bullet out when he gets here. With all due respect, Colonel, let me do my work," she said, then ignored the older woman.

Singh crawled outside and waited for her night vision to slowly adjust, watching the Invy orbital soar through the clear summer sky. The moon, a sliver hanging in the eastern sky, showed lights in its shadowed part. They had been growing over the last five years, and she wondered what the Invy were doing up there. Occasionally a fusion drive flared brightly, a ship making a course adjustment, and she cursed the aliens that had denied her people a place in the stars.

"Makes you wonder how we're going to beat them, doesn't it?" asked Master Sergeant Agostine.

She didn't answer for a moment, then said, "I'm going to get on my horse and ride into battle like I did today, and kick their asses."

He laughed and said, "I'm not even sure a Dragon HAS an ass!"

"Nick, why the hell am I out here chasing numb-nuts around?" There was a note of weariness in her voice. "I should be back at Raven Rock, overseeing final preparations for the attack."

"Dalpe's got it under control, and you gave the orders to the scouts already. Besides, if he doesn't get to where he's going soon, we're not going to make it back in time ourselves."

A runner had been sent to the coast, to speak with a dolphin, who in turned relayed a message to one of the Russian ballistic submarines waiting in the Atlantic. They were to hold station outside

Galveston, and be ready to move the scouts back to the Chesapeake Bay area. It would cut weeks off their travel time.

They were both quiet for a moment, then Agostine asked, "So where do you think he's going?"

"Maybe back to Colorado to get his medical records and file a claim with the VA."

"Yeah, that's a battle I wouldn't want to fight. Seriously, though."

"I think he's headed back to Cheyenne Mountain. There's something there that Warren needs, though last time I saw it, it wasn't really a mountain anymore. Just a really deep hole in the ground. It was one of the few places the Invy landed on their initial assault, sent in a whole regiment of Wolverines to clear the place out."

Though she couldn't see it, she knew that the veteran soldier was thinking about it. She had all their personnel records, and knew that he had been at the fight to protect the CEF Space Command Headquarters.

"How's the leg?" she asked him.

"Riding a horse is easier than walking across the entire damn country."

"Amen to that, brother!" said a burly figure in the starlight. "I got the report on the laser, but we were hauling ass as soon as I heard the gunfire. How is he?"

"Took a 9mm from a submachine gun at close range, and the bullet is still in his shoulder, just under the skin. Probably shitty reloaded ammo," answered Singh, "and maybe glanced off the bone. Brit is in there now with him, and I gave him some nanos immediately. That was two hours ago."

"OK, I'll get to work. Infection's what we have to worry about." The medic disappeared into the tent, and the two of them walked further away to continue the conversation.

"Nick, do you think we can pull this off? Think someday you'll be able to have your farm, and make a bunch of rug rats with Ms. O'Neill?"

"I. AM. NOT. INVOLVED. WITH. SERGEANT. O'NEILL!"

Singh grinned in the darkness at the NCO's tone. She liked to tease him when she could, it kept him humble.

"ANYWAY ..." he continued, "Honestly, Rachel, I don't know. What I am concerned about is our infiltration on the DC spaceport. Six of us, to get a couple of pilots onto a base, cover them while they take off to go pick up assault troops, and then exfiltration? It's going to be suicide."

"One shuttle, one pilot. The others are going to be taken care of by Major Ikeda and his team in Japan, and Captain MacGregor in Scotland. Gives us a shorter intercept time."

"Well, now I feel much better!" he answered sarcastically. "If we were going after three in one place, the element of surprise would help, but if there is ANY missed timing on three sides of the world, the Invy will be onto it in an instant."

"General Arkady said it was an acceptable risk, not putting all our eggs in one basket, and I agree with her."

"Well, it's our asses, not hers."

"That's not fair, Nick," she said, her voice hard. "You know the price she paid."

"Her life. Hopefully not mine. Or Brits. Or anyone else on the team."

She sighed with exasperation. "What's really bugging you, Sergeant?"

He waited, then said, "Officially, or unofficially?"

"If you have a valid critique of the plan, then say it. I trust your experience."

"Well, since you asked, officially it's the best plan we can come up with, given METT-T."

"Mission, Enemy, Terrain, Troops, and Time," she said, almost chanting it. "Yes, I think it is, but unofficially?"

Agostine had a good relationship with his commander, much more like partners than leader/subordinate, but he was uncomfortable complaining. Still, he'd opened his mouth, so out with it.

"Unofficially, for the last nine years, after we came out of hiding in the bases, every mission you've given us has been a 'go do this' and you never told me *how* to do it. Now I have boy wonder there telling me the exact timing to infiltrate an enemy base. I'm waiting for him to tell me exactly *how* we should do it."

"Nick, what do you know about Operation Brightstar?" she asked.

Chapter 34

"Not much. I'm not cleared for it," he answered honestly. "It had something to do with taking really smart kids and training them to be the best tactical and strategic planners we could produce. Sounds like a bunch of bullshit to me."

"Well, that was the cover story. What they really did was meld their brains with computer processors. They called it 'the Implant'. It allowed them to have instant access to terabytes of information, communicate directly with the AIs, and think about three times faster than the average human."

"You're shitting me," he exclaimed. "That knucklehead? He just got himself shot today!"

"Give him a break, he's got a lot on his mind, pun intended, and he was never trained for what WE do. There's a huge difference between thinking up a plan in an instant to maneuver your platoon, company, fleet, whatever, and knowing how to react when you're staring down the barrel of a gun. Hell," she said, "half the shooting we do is based on muscle memory more than anything."

He knew that; it was why they trained so hard. He didn't have to think to know that Doc would go right when he went left, or that Ziv could nail a running man at a thousand meters.

"I can see that, I guess. Still…"

"You will have complete tactical control on the ground, Captain Agostine."

He made a low laugh in the starlight. "I'm not taking your promotion, Rachel. I'm an NCO, I'll stay an NCO, thanks."

"Someday."

"Someday I'll be sitting pretty on a farm on the shore of Lake Champlain and won't hear nothing but the corn growing."

Neither had much to say for a while, just sat there and watched the stars. Eventually the Master Sergeant brought up the immediate future.

"I think you should head back east, as fast as possible. Take the rest of the team with you, I'll keep O'Neill with me."

"I bet you will."

"Ugh, no. She's Combat Lifesaver trained, has some medical knowledge, she can keep an eye on Warren, watch for infection. Doc is my second in command, he needs to take the team on reconnaissance to DC. We'll get boy wonder where he needs to go, and send word back through pigeon from the Main Force unit in Denver. Who is the commander there?"

"Lieutenant Colonel Peckham. Good man. Tell him I send my regards."

Agostine was still troubled. He sat and thought hard about what was to happen in the next couple of months. Warren was an enigma, outside his experience. He thought in terms of tactics, not strategy. All of his experience was in direct action, putting steel on target, letting others deal with the big picture, and the why. He cared about his people, but he was tired.

"What do you want me to do with Warren?"

"It's General Warren. He's our commander now. You don't do anything with him, except what he tells you to do, and you keep him alive. And you don't have to like him, either."

"Can do, Ma'am." She could hear the hardness in his voice.

"Oh, it's Ma'am now, is it? Nick, we don't have to like what we do, we just have to do it."

He grunted, and said, "I didn't like it when the Wolverines ate my leg, either, but I did what I had to do."

"We all pay our price and soldier on," she answered.

"Well, endgame is in sight. If we fail, the Invy are going to scorch the Earth with that virus. We're taking the lives of the entire human race in our hands, Rachel."

"The alternative is what? Endless slavery? You know what it's like, being their slave, don't you?"

"Time to change the subject. I wish Drummond had been able to make it through. He wasn't a bad kid, just misguided. I can't but think that we could have saved him."

Singh shrugged, and said, "The A Team in his village had him pegged as soon as he started talking to that asshole, the Greenie leader there. We had to let it play through, to get Curtis to come out in the open."

Agostine spit on the ground, an indication of how much the political stuff disgusted him. It was why he stayed away from headquarters as much as he could. "Do you think that guy is actually a threat? The Greenie, Carlyle."

"As soon as he gets too big for his britches, the Invy will slap him down. Especially when they somehow find out that he used to be high ranking military."

"He was?"

Singh laughed. "Of course not, Nick. I swear, you're so naïve sometimes. Of course not, but convincing documents will just happen to appear in the wrong place. The Greens will never be organized. Neither us nor the Invy will let them."

"Too much bullshit for me. I'm going to see how things are with Warren."

"Nick," the Colonel said, "I know you don't like him, but wherever he's going, it's important. Make sure he gets there."

"It's always important, and it's always the guys like us who pay the price," he answered, bitterness in his voice. She had nothing to say in answer to that.

—

He met Doc Hamilton coming out of the tent, and asked how Warren was.

"Left shoulder is going to be useless for the foreseeable future. He's going to be OK, but he'll need physical therapy, maybe reconstructive surgery for the tendons. You know it ain't like the movies, bullets fuck you up."

"Can he travel?"

"Ain't nothing wrong with his legs or his ass."

Agostine took that as an affirmative, and ducked past him into the tent. The General sat there as O'Neill finished bandaging his shoulder.

"Brit, we roll first light. You, me and Boy Wonder here."

Warren glared at him, and the veteran NCO stared right back. "General, or whatever you are, I'll get you to where you're going, and I'll put my life on the line to do it. But when we get there, so help me, I will put a bullet in your head if what you're after isn't worth it."

"Fair enough. I'm not going to pretend that I'm some kind of hardcore grunt like you, or Sergeant O'Neill here, but trust me, I know what I'm doing."

Chapter 35

Colorado Springs

The brilliant dawn painted the mountains in a blaze of red, then pink, then gold. Even more than a decade later, dust in the atmosphere gave rise to beautiful sunrises and sunsets. Brittany O'Neill knelt to face the sun, and let her red hair flow down unbound to her waist. She started chanting slowly, hands clasped in front of her.

"What the hell is she doing, some kind of Wiccan shit?" asked Warren. In the two weeks it had taken them to get close to Cheyenne Mountain, his shoulder had healed enough that he could move around without a sling.

"She's a devout Roman Catholic. Just her morning prayers," answered Agostine.

The woman stopped chanting, stood up, and yelled out to the mountain side, "Hot damn, it's great to be alive!"

In front of them stood a mountain that was covered with impact craters. Across the valley were the rusted remnants of both Human and Invy armored vehicles; scattered across the plain were perfectly round lakes, craters filled with rain water over the last eleven years.

"I didn't see the battle, you know. I was in a cell," said Warren, a lost look on his face.

Agostine stood next to him, looking outward also, and said quietly, "I was there. See that line of trenches over there, right up by the entrance? That's where my men died. I was a Staff Sergeant, Fourth Infantry Division. My Bradley took a hit from a plasma cannon, went through it like the armor was made of tinfoil. We were dismounted at that point, heavy weapons team."

Warren said nothing, just let him talk. "See that wrecked Invy Tank? Third from the left? About two hundred meters out. I took that out. Two more, but I can't remember where."

"You know it was hopeless, right? We were way overmatched."

The anger coming off the older man was unmistakable; he seemed to be fighting hard to hold himself in check. "Not on the ground, we weren't, man for man. Our weapons hurt them, pretty damn badly. If we had had air cover, if you had done your fucking job…"

"Yeah, I know. I tried, Sergeant, I really did, but there wasn't any way. Maybe it was hubris, I don't know. But once we lost the high ground, it was over."

Agostine pointed at the craters in the mountain. "Do you know why they finally did an orbital bombardment? Because we stopped them cold. Fought tooth and nail, killed thousands of them, and finally they pulled back and let us have it. Over three hundred and seventy-five thousand men and women died here that week, General, and you bastards in that mountain shut the doors on us when the orbital strikes started." For a while, he seemed to be back there, reliving it, and Warren said nothing. What *could* he say?

O'Neill came up and put her arms around Agostine, hugging him tightly. He shrugged her off and said, "Well, let's get this over with. There's an Invy garrison directly across from the main entrance, and they still use the airfield sometimes. It's going to be a very long and slow process to infiltrate there. If that's where we're going, since you haven't told us yet."

"*We* aren't going anywhere, Master Sergeant," said Warren. "I'm going down there, and you're not going to stop me. I don't want to put any more lives at risk, so I'm giving you two a direct order to let me go."

O'Neill started to move her hand towards her gun, but Agostine waved her off, and she merely folded her arms across her chest.

"I appreciate the sentiment, General, but I have my orders. If we let anything happen to you, Colonel Singh is going to have our hides."

Warren didn't waver, just looked at them stolidly. "Be that as it may, Sergeant, this is something I have to do myself."

"Why?" asked O'Neill, her one good eye gazing at him steadily.

"Because … it's too complicated to explain."

"We have all day," said Agostine, and he sat down on a tree stump, taking up a listening pose. "This should be good."

Warren started forward, and the redhead whipped her pistol out, pointing it directly at Warren's face from ten feet away. He flinched backwards, expecting the shot, but the SIG just stayed there, rock solid in her grip.

"Nick, what do you want me to do?" she said, "Think he's going to talk to his Invy friends down there in the valley?"

"I doubt it," he answered. "Probably just running away again to some hidey hole he knew from before the war. Probably doesn't think we have a shot in hell of beating them. Isn't that right, General? Going to sit it out while we get slaughtered?"

"We don't, honestly. Those orbitals are going to knock those missiles right out of the sky before they can impact," answered Warren. "I wish I could take both of you with me, but the person I'm going to meet won't talk to me if you're there."

"And what does this person have to do with winning the war?" asked O'Neill. "Can I shoot him now, Nick?"

"No. Let him talk."

"He's a … a hacker, I guess you could say. The only way we can beat them is to somehow get into their networks and disable them. If anyone can do it, it's him. If he's still alive."

O'Neill lowered her gun and said, "The Invy networks are quantum based, use a different coding language, and are encrypted. There's no way."

"Well, I have to try. Even if it means getting killed going through there, and I don't want your deaths on my conscience."

Agostine stood up, looked at his fellow scout, and said, "So be it. Let him go, Brit. Pack it up, we can catch the sub in three weeks if we haul ass. It's only a month until D-Day."

He watched them go, following their progress until they disappeared into the forest, taking his horse with them. Warren looked ruefully at his own feet, missing the horse already, and started down into the valley.

The road he followed hadn't seen a maintenance crew in more than a decade, and he tried hard to stay in the center of the pavement, avoiding the crumbling edges. Around the first switchback, though, evidence of the battle started to appear. A skull here, a rusting weapon there, smashed vehicles with holes drilled through by plasma bolts. With grim satisfaction, he noted that some of the skulls weren't human, and that several of the wrecks were of Invy manufacture.

By the end of the day, he had made it down to the main battlefield, twice having to take cover from Invy aircraft flying overhead. He ignored the various signs in English and Spanish warning that the area was forbidden, backtracking the route he had taken when he escaped his cell, heading east to return home. It seemed like a journey back in time, and he moved forward almost eagerly.

Too eagerly, it turned out. Lost in his musings, he walked directly into sight of an Invy patrol, settling down for the night. The first he knew of it was the plasma bolt that shattered the ground at his feet, and the harsh, amplified electronic voice ordering him to stop.

Chapter 36

"Well, he didn't make it very far, did he? Dumbass."

Agostine watched from behind the tree stump, five hundred meters away. "Brit, you know what we're going to have to do."

"Yes," she answered. "Nick, if anything happens to you, I'm going to kill him."

"We'll be fine. Hit them hard and fast, there's only four of them."

She checked the loads on her pistols, two SIG P250 .357 automatics with ceramic sabot rounds, for penetrating Invy armor.

"I'd kill for my shotgun right now," she muttered.

The Master Sergeant offered her his P-90, but she turned it down. "I'll stick to what I know. Any chance we can just let him die?"

"No. He needs to get where he's going. They're bedding down for the night; one sentry. Thank God they're on foot, an APC AI would nail us from two hundred meters out. Hand me that scent masker."

The both doused each other liberally, even though they would approach from downwind. The movement would be excruciatingly slow, because the one sentry would be wearing thermal NVGs.

In the fading light, they confirmed that Warren was cuffed and stretched out on the ground, alongside two other prisoners. As they watched, one of the Wolverines grabbed a prisoner by her long hair, extended his ripping claw, and cut her throat. Another one held a cup under the gash and collected her blood, and then they started skinning her while a third lit a fire.

It wasn't anything they hadn't seen before, but O'Neill dug her nails into Agostine's arm to stop him from charging forward. "Slow is steady, steady is fast, Nick," she whispered in his ear. She reached over in the growing darkness and wiped the anger from his face, then kissed him gently.

"In another world, Nick, we're going to live a long and happy life, and it's going to be soon. Don't forget that. Now let's go, old man." He relaxed under her grip, and she let go, but not right away. Her touch said more than any words between them ever could.

They first circled wide of the encampment, swinging far off the road to the south, almost crawling from fallen tree to sunken ditch, timing their movement to when the lone guard turned away. Their chameleon suits would have hid them, but they also generated tremendous amounts of sweat and body heat, and weren't ideal for avoiding an IR capable sentry. Instead, they took advantage of every bit of terrain possible, getting to within fifty meters.

The fire backlit the sentry as he turned towards them, four-foot-high silhouette showing darkly, except for the red glowing eyes of the alien night vision tech. Agostine slid a flash bang grenade out of his pocket and worked the retaining pin out, then laid his free hand on O'Neill's arm. He pressed downward, counting, one, two, and then threw the grenade into the center of the camp.

It detonated with a deafening CRACK and a blinding flash of light; both rose off the ground and charged forward, each firing at the sentry.

The wolverine went down with a howl, plasma rifle discharging into the sky, and they switched aim to the others, who had instantly rolled to different positions and returned fire into the night. First one, then another caught successive rounds from the two humans as they ran closer, but the third shifted his fire in the direction of their shots. The needle thin bolts of plasma whipped past them, and Agostine heard his partner grunt and gasp.

He ignored her and turned his P-90 to the last remaining Invy, emptying the magazine, and then quickly dropping it in its sling and drawing his pistol. He got up and ran through the campsite, putting two rounds in the head of each alien corpse, then ran back to where O'Neill sprawled on the ground.

She lay there, holding her hands to her stomach, just under her body armor, face turned up to the sky. Agostine knew the damage the wound had done, the jet of plasma burning its way through vital organs, superheating the fluids inside her abdomen, causing massive tissue damage, exiting out the other side.

"Oh, f-f-f-fuck me, Nick, this f-f-fucking hurts!" she moaned. He quickly dug into her med kit and pulled out a morphine injector, and jabbed into her rib cage. The needle slid under her skin, and after what seemed like an eternity, the pain seemed to leave her face.

She reached up and touched the stubble on his cheek, staring with her one crystal blue eye, as if trying to memorize his features, and wiped at his tears. Her other hand squeezed his gently, and she whispered, "I was going to go to the stars, Nick. They're so beautiful. And kids, we were going to have a lot of kids…"

"Hush," he whispered, and held her tightly, bitter, salty tears running down his face and mixing with the blood that had trickled out of the corner of her mouth. After a time, the hand holding his fell limply away.

Master Sergeant Nicholas Agostine sat there, cradling the still body, and wept in harsh, wracking sobs. Eventually he laid her gently down on the ground, and stood up, walking towards where Warren sat, back against a tree. The other prisoner had caught a round in the face, and was slumped over next to him.

His first kick caught the handcuffed man in the face, knocking him over, and it was followed by a flurry of punches and kicks that turned the General's face into a bloody mask. He made no effort to defend himself, merely curled into a ball and took it. The scout rained blows and kicks on his body, cursing him over and over.

Finally, energy spent, Agostine drew his pistol and held it against the man's head. "Tell me to do it. Please, order me. You stupid piece of shit." His words were ice cold, and his eyes, red and raw from weeping, held no emotion now.

"You do what you have to do, Sergeant," said Warren through bloody, split lips. After a long minute, the NCO sat back, and placed the pistol in his own mouth, closing his eyes.

"Is that what she would have wanted?"

Agostine took the pistol out of his mouth, slowly putting it back in its holster, then answered, "I'll never know, will I? I hope you burn in hell."

Chapter 37

On the far side of the shattered mountain, David Warren limped along through the night. He had left the scout NCO far behind, Agostine heading southward after cutting off the handcuffs. His mind raced with thoughts, feeling the guilt of O'Neill's death. Victoria, Jeremy, O'Neill, they all weighed on him, far more than the billions of dead from the war.

His mind raced with battle plans, status of forces, statistics on the enemy, but his faster thinking only made it worse. Agostine had been right, he decided, to curse him. David Warren, despite the initial resurgence of spirit once he put on his General stars again, was again close to becoming a beaten man.

The truth was, he didn't know how to find what he was looking for. The concealed exit he had used was just that, concealed, and although he knew he was in the right spot, generally, eleven years of growth had covered it over. Despair burned through him like an Invy plasma beam.

Behind him, the valley swarmed with Invy patrol craft. Occasionally, one would dart downward and fire into the forest. He was sure that their horses were long dead, though Agostine had rode out of there like a bat out of hell. None seemed to notice him, though, as he walked slowly and painfully along the road, and he didn't think to wonder why. Who knew why the Invy did what they did? It just seemed so, so random. Gotta keep going, he thought, gotta keep going.

He fell down on the road, and lay there as the sun rose over the rim of the eastern ridge. It crawled across his body, slowly warming him. As he lay there, face pressed against the pavement, a bug walked in front of his face. Then another. Both stood in front of his eyes; they looked like cockroaches, similar to the ones he had seen at CEF HQ.

One walked up closer, and then each eye started to blink, alternating one green, then the other red. Tiny lights. Drones. He staggered to his feet, and they scuttled off down the road, the pair soon being joined by another, then another, until there were more than a dozen, forming an arrow.

"So goddamned predictable," he muttered. "Like some kind of crappy sci-fi novel. Damn you Hal, if it is you. You read too much."

They eventually led him deep into the scrub brush and through a small ravine, and he remembered the way from there. As soon as he entered, the drones scattered, some flying away and others scuttling off.

He thought back to the night, eleven years ago, when he had come out this way. It had been dark, then, but the mountain had been backlit by the rain of fire that was devastating the ground forces. The ground had shaken with each successive strike, and to be honest, he had run, more scared than he had ever been in his life. He had joined in the stream of soldiers fleeing the battlefield, losing himself in a panicked mass of humanity that had slowly dispersed into the devastated countryside.

The doorway looked like solid rock, and Warren took a deep breath, reached around a small outcropping, turned a protruding rock, and pushed. It swung open easily, but the air that came out was foul and smelled of long ago death. Taking a deep breath of fresh air and pulling his t-shirt up over his face, he turned on his flashlight, pulled out the pistol Agostine had given him, and descended into the darkness, pulling the door shut behind him.

His flash only illuminated the corridor for about thirty feet, but it was fairly clean, no footprints or animal tracks in the dust. He followed it down a long curving ramp to another doorway, one he knew opened to the main floor of the old NORAD HQ. This he approached with trepidation, afraid of what was on the other side.

It took all his strength to push it open; it was concealed from view on the other side, seemingly part of the wall. Hal had shown him this way out before he shut himself down, wiping his sentience out when he wiped the internet and destroyed the cloud.

Warren didn't know what he hoped for. The drones seemed to have some very basic intelligence; perhaps collectively they had some greater intelligence. Why, though, had they formed the letters H-A-L at Raven Rock? The AI had inhabited the internet, his body part of the servers that ran it. When he had taken the net down, and wiped all electronic records, Hal he effectively destroyed himself. It had been a bitter goodbye to a good friend; one he had run countless simulations with, and had long conversations with about strategy and history.

After he had been sprung from his cell by Rhuta and Smith, his two classmates on the Battle Staff, and their Delta escort, they had a running gun battle with a detachment of Wolverines, leading to the nightmare he'd had over and over ever since. The Delta sergeant shoving him into the doorway to the deserted Command Center, and Warren sitting at the console one last time, to give the execute order to Hal.

He had fled through a series of interconnecting tunnels that brought him back to the main chamber, moving through the shadows from cover to cover as the last of the defenders died. They were headquarters troops, rear detachment types, but they took more than they lost, and in the end, they died with their boots on.

All along the floors were scattered bones, still clad in the remnants of uniforms, burned in many places by plasma weapons. The buildings, still sitting on their shocks, were holed and shattered. Twice he started when rats ran past him, and it took him almost twenty minutes to find the door to the Command Center. It was shattered, hanging sideways on broken hinges, the armor peeled back by demolition charges. To one side was a human skeleton with a shattered arm, still clutching a large knife. Entangled with it were the bones of a wolverine, and another was stretched out at his feet.

He crouched down and gently detached the dog tags that were moldering among the bones and read them before he slipped them into his pocket. ELLIS, VINCENT J. "See you on Fiddler's Green, Sergeant Ellis," he whispered to his last remaining bodyguard, and stepped in through the shattered door.

Chapter 38

South China Sea, three weeks later.

The *CEF Vermont* sat on the sandy bottom of the South China Sea, five kilometers outside what was once Ho Chi Minh City, and before that, Saigon. Captain Larken thought briefly of her great grandfather, Chief Boson's Mate Eric Larken, who had been killed the day after her grandmother had been born back in the states. She had a picture of him, all of twenty-two years old, taped to the bulkhead in her cabin.

She wondered what he would have thought of Major Ikeda's mission. Even as she paced around the Conn, worrying that they weren't deep enough to stay hidden, Chief Ball came back from forward.

"They're away, Captain. Now we just wait."

"Yes, Chief, we wait. That's what we bubbleheads do, right?"

"Yes'm. I'm just glad that thing is off the boat." He took a rag and wiped his bald head; she had never seen him so nervous.

"Chief, we have over twenty A-SAT missiles sitting in their launch tubes, nuke armed Tomahawks, and three nuclear armed M-98 torps. You're freaking out over one loose one."

"Those are properly secured. That one wasn't. Just makes me nervous on my boat, is all."

She laughed and said, "It's MY boat, Chief."

"That's just a fiction us Chiefs allow you to believe, Ma'am, to assuage your delicate egos."

"Careful you don't hurt your brain with those big words, Chief!"

Major Ikeda let his head gently break the surface, glancing around through the night. Beside him the diver from the *Vermont* surfaced slightly and squeezed his shoulder. From here on out, it was on his team to deliver the device. His wished for a firearm, but if they engaged in any kind of fight with a patrol, and Invy bodies were found with gunshot wounds, they would blow the whole operation. There weren't any other humans within a few thousand miles.

They had debated leaving the device on the floor of the bay, but Captain Larken had argue against it. Her view was that seawater might affect the timer, which was set for H-hour, and that the backup radio detonator might not reach into the water.

So they were going to drag it up the beach and bury it. The entire team was clad in sealed wetsuits with rebreathers; they risked horrible death from the 30-degree virus if they showed any exposed skin. It was incredibly hot, and raining. What was good cover for a raid also made for more miserable conditions.

He motioned for his flankers to move out, and they disappeared into the ruins of the old city. In the distance, two kilometers away, the lights of the Invy settlement glowed. At his feet were thousands of bones; the infected had come down to the shore to find relief, but had only found death.

Cursing inwardly as his mask started to fog up, Ikeda adjusted his air flow and set to digging. The device was shielded, so there shouldn't be any leakage of radiation to set off Invy detectors. Not in the week they had left.

The nuke weighed almost four hundred pounds, and had a yield of about five hundred kilotons. Detonated on the ground, even if the blast didn't destroy the lab and communications complex, about two miles away, they were very carefully placing it upwind. Hopefully enough radiation would coat the facility to make it unapproachable and un-useable, but the primary target was to disrupt the Invy air defenses so the *Virginia's* Tomahawks could deliver a knockout blow.

He heard a harsh, barked word from his left hand flanker, "DRAGON!" and Ikeda and the rest of his men instantly went to ground. Corporal Misui appeared from the brush, holding up one finger on his right hand, then two on his left. One Dragon and two Wolverines. Some high placed administrator from the city out to enjoy the heat and the rain. He cursed under his breath, and they all lay quietly, waiting. The roadway was fifty meters from the beach, but there was also a turn off that led onto the sand and muck. *Why the hell was this stupid Invy out here in the middle of the night?*

The kanji of bad karma cursed them again as the three aliens turned off the road and walked slowly onto the beach, the Dragon unbuckling his golden armor with a hiss and making directly for the water. His two guards stopped, causing Ikeda to say a silent prayer that the rain had masked their scent, and that they were complacent this far from human settlement. He also hoped it had washed away the tracks the heavy sled had made as they dragged it up.

No luck. The Wolverine closest to the wood line where they hid smelled something, and his head rose as he sniffed the air. Sergeant Shimada, who was closest to them, whipped out his sword and dashed across the sand at them.

In combat, when things go bad, they often go really bad. The Wolverine reacted incredibly quickly, holding up a paw to his partner and extending his ripping claws. It ducked under Shimada's swing and gutted him, cutting upwards through his wet suit and coming out of his back. The creature howled as the rest of the team rose from the woods and charged, all four of them drawing various blades.

Ikeda's right flanker hit the other Wolverine from behind, just as it raised its plasma rifle, sticking it through the neck with his knife. Both fell to the sand in a flurry of cuts, spilling dark blood on the sand.

Ikeda ignored the fight between the remaining guard and his three men, and charged down the beach after the Dragon, which was swimming quickly away. The heat generated inside his wetsuit quickly overcame him, and he fell to his knees, trying to breathe, and watching the Dragon disappear into the darkness.

Despair washed over him like a wave from the Pacific. Red Dawn was blown. He turned back to his men, and saw that only two were still standing, while Corporal Misui was down on one knee, trying frantically to patch a tear in his wetsuit.

When Ikeda approached, the younger man stood up and bowed. Nothing was said, Ikeda just returned the bow, then reached out and gripped the man's hand for a long minute. Misui took off his helmet, and breathed in the deadly air deeply, knowing that he was infected already.

"It is good to feel wind in your face when looking at death," said the soldier peacefully. "You have been a good commander, Major. Please tell my wife I was thinking of her, and give my daughter this when she is old enough to understand," he said, handed Ikeda his knife, then turned and bowed once more to each of his fellow soldiers. Picking up another knife, he walked down into the water, swimming outward into the pre-dawn.

Ikeda and the remaining soldiers quickly dug two pits in the sand, carrying on with the mission, even though they all knew it was doomed. Into one pit, they placed the bodies of the two guards, and into another, the bodies of their two comrades, then smoothed the sand until there was nothing to show. Ikeda detailed one man to bury the blood trails, and then he and the other continued to dig the hole for the nuke.

As he dug, the Major clamped down hard on his disappointment, and pushed the grief over losing his men to the side. They had served together before the invasion, and he had only lost one teammate in all the years since.

When they were done, there was no trace of the buried weapon or the bodies, or evidence of the fight. The golden armor of the Dragon was in the pit with the Wolverines, but their plasma rifles went with the retreating scouts. Hopefully the Dragon would drown, and the missing Invy would be written off as victims of the jungle.

They walked into the surf and swam outward until the brackish river water closed over their heads, then dove downward. A sleek torpedo shaped animal appeared out of the darkness, followed by another, pulling one of the *Vermont's* divers. Ikeda and his men hooked on, and they were quickly pulled into deeper water to meet up with the SEAL Delivery Vehicle. When they plugged into the intercom, the diver asked how it went.

"We were compromised, several Invy stumbled across the site and one got away into the ocean," he answered, despair finally creeping into his voice. He was brought out of it by the woman's laughter as they sped along in the growing light.

"Is that where that came from?" she asked, and pointed through the darkness. Another dolphin swam closer, dragging the heavy body of the Dragon, shoving it this way and that in a game that they seemed to enjoy immensely. Occasionally one would push it towards the surface, and another would shove it back down.

"It'll wash up eventually; every now and then the Dolphins drown one for fun. When we get back to the ship, I'll ask Cicero why they hate them so much, and he'll give me some bullshit answer, like they always do." She laughed again, and said in her thick Southern American accent, "Everything is a damn puzzle or a game to them!"

H-71:20

Chapter 39

Nick Agostine strode purposefully through the night, headed towards the Invy base outside Washington. The Russian sub had dropped him off deep inside Chesapeake Bay, and he thanked the boatmen in their own language as the paddled away.

Now, he was to meet the rest of the team in a basement, only two miles from the base itself. For the millionth time, he replayed the events of that damned night over in his head, second guessing himself. Every move that he had made played back over and over; what kept sticking in there was the awful grunt that she had made when she was hit. That sound would haunt him forever.

He had spent two days hiding under the rusted remains of an Abrams tank, fearing that any moment, a passing Wolverine patrol would smell him out. Instead, they had done gun runs on any heat spot that they saw, killing countless deer and other wild animals. *Environmentalists my ass,* he thought.

At the end of the second day, he slowly maneuvered his way back up the mountain side, and when he finally crested the ridge, he whistled, hard, and waited. An hour later, only one of the horses showed, and his heart clenched painfully when he saw that it was Brit's.

The ride back to the Texas coast had been a nightmare, pushing the horse from one friendly homestead to another, and he had barely made the rendezvous before the sub had to leave. The following week he had spent restlessly walking the 'forest', the green painted missile tubes, doing countless pushups and sit ups.

Now he moved easily, knowing that one of the team had him in their sights. The veteran NCO turned off the broken highway at a certain spot, moving down side streets amid ruined housing. He ignored the passing drones that buzzed down and looked him in the face, then flew away. What did they care about one lone traveler, whose face had never been recorded before?

He climbed in through the root cellar doors that led to the team hideout, and was greeted by Doc Hamilton. The burly medic reached out and grabbed him in a bone crushing hug, then let go. Word of Brit's death had reached them by whale song as soon as Agostine had set foot on the Russian ship. Reynolds started to say something, but her boss held up his hand.

"We have a mission to focus on. What's the status of the team?" he asked, ignoring the pained look on Reynolds' face.

"Ziv is asleep after watch. Boyd you saw on your way in, or more likely you didn't see him."

"I didn't; good. Who else?"

"Colonel Singh assigned two more, to bring us to seven, and we have one pilot to babysit, Major Hollister."

Agostine knew the pilot, and respected her. She had often accompanied teams out into the field, and was almost as good at sneaking as they were. "Who else?"

"Specialist Redshirt and Chief Yassir. Singh sent us the best that she could. They're out doing recon on the base."

"OK then. Change of plans. I'm going in alone with Hollister. You all will get me as far as the perimeter, then provide overwatch and covering fire. You are NOT going into the base with me."

"Nick..." Hamilton started to say, "the Main Force elements are-" He stopped when he saw the look on his friend's face.

"I know what you're going to say, so don't. You think I'm out of my head over Brit's death, but I'm not. I think any more than two will only increase our chances of compromise."

"Rachel isn't going to go for that," Doc shot back.

"She can fire me when this is done. I'm here, so I'm calling the shots. Where is she, anyway?"

Reynolds and Hamilton both looked at each other, but said nothing.

"Out with it," said their commander, angrily.

"She's going in with us, and will be here early this morning."

Agostine groaned, and muttered, "Ahhhh shit. Is Major Hollister awake?"

Hamilton watched the wheels spin in his friend's head, and knew that, no matter what he said, Nick Agostine was on a suicide mission.

Chapter 40

Deep inside the former CEF Space Command, General David Warren was feeling despair, and hunger. His rations had given out three days ago, and his water earlier today. The darkness and remnant of death pressed down heavily on him, and his frustration grew deeper and deeper.

It was H – 23:00; in little less than a day Red Dawn would kick off, and he sat alone in the deep dark, useless. The hopes that he had, that something still remained here that they could use against the Invy, lay locked behind one last door, warped and stuck shut. The drones had disappeared under the sill, and still occasionally came out, looked at him imploringly, and went back in.

He sat there, squeezing the recharge handle on the flashlight, and ventured out into the open space one more time, looking for something to pry the door open with. As he walked, he desperately scanned the database he'd updated at Raven Rock, trying to come up with something, anything that might spark an idea.

Finding nothing, he went back to the doorway, which was hidden inside an old supply room. He thought it led down to a sub-basement, almost a thousand feet deep into the core of the mountain, and provided access to the ansible communications, as well as servers for the base computer systems. It made sense that the drones would come from there. A random shot from a heavy weapons system, fired from outside the room, had punched a hole in the wall and jarred the door - not enough to reveal it, but enough to throw it off balance. The past two weeks had been spent trying everything he could to pry it open.

Now, he looked down at the collection of weapons he had picked up. Several M-6 carbines, all rusted past use. A half dozen grenades; he had already tried one on the door, and got nothing but a cut from ricocheting shrapnel.

The last weapon was an Invy plasma pistol, which he hadn't thought to look at too closely, figuring that it would be in the same condition as the rifles. In desperation, he picked it up and wiped the dirt and dried blood off of it, stood back behind the entrance to the room, pointed it at the door, and pulled the trigger.

To his surprise, plasma ripped out of the barrel and hit the door squarely, burning a hole through the hardened steel. Waiting for it to cool, he finally approached and shone the flashlight on the mark it made. A tiny stream of steel had melted its way down, and there was a needle thin hole through the door. Warren noticed a small amber light glowing on the top of the pistol, only visible while looking down the sights, and cursed, then stopped. From the hole shone a steady beam of light, and he put his eye up to it. Beyond was another corridor, the electric light was blinding after so long in the darkness with only the weak flashlight.

His implant provided, unbidden, a set of specs for the weapon in his hand. Eighty shot capacity, and the low energy light came on with ten shots left. At five, it turned to red. He groaned; less than ten shots would do nothing except put a few little holes in the door. Then he had a thought, and raced his way through the information the Raven Rock R & D people had provided on captured weapons.

The energy for the plasma weapons was stored in a crystalline structure that held hydrogen and anti-hydrogen suspended. Firing the weapon broke the matrix, and the energy involved was used to create a directional beam of plasma. Earth scientists still had no idea how it worked, even how the resultant energy was transferred to the plasma, but Warren didn't need that now. What he needed was an explosion. A big one. If he could destroy the structure that held the remaining shots in place, it could, in theory, cause them to detonate all at once, and not transfer their energy into a directional beam.

Hurriedly ransacking the supply room, he found an old, dried up roll of 100 MPH tape, and said a silent prayer to the gods of logistics. Removing the magazine, he taped one of the grenades to it. Then, using the old formula of *p=plenty*, he said screw it and taped together the rest of them. Then, very carefully, he set the bundle at the base of the door, taped it to the steel, and hooked his last grenade onto the tape. A length of 550 cord barely fell twenty feet short of the doorway to the outside, but he would have to chance it. If only one of these M-6s had worked, but they were junk, and he didn't trust his own shooting with a pistol from far enough away.

When the dust cleared, his ears were still ringing from the combined blasts, and he could barely breathe from the impact on his lungs. Warren stood up and walked forward to where the door still stood. Now though, it was buckled and bent, and the lights still flickered on the other side. He stripped off his body armor and, barely able to make it, squeezed his way inside.

The corridor beyond swept downward in a steep spiral, making him lean forward as he walked. The drones reappeared, almost comforting, and led him further and further into the depths.

H- 4:52

Chapter 41

Outside Loch Brea Invy Spaceport, Scotland.

"For it's Tommy this, an' Tommy that, an 'Chuck him out, the brute!' But it's 'Saviour of 'is country' when the guns begin to shoot!" muttered Private Thomas Adkins as he looked through his rifle scope. He wasn't watching any of the enemy; instead he was gauging wind speed and direction between himself and the sensor pod mounted on a tower high above the base. In his hands he held a .50 caliber rifle with high explosive rounds.

"That's why your mother named you Tommy, my lad. So you can die for your King and Country!" said Corporal Vlonski as he lay next to him. The polish immigrant still spoke with a heavy accent, but was as laconic as his native English counterparts.

"I bloody hope not, but if I do, the girls in Inverness will burn down the Invy town all on their own," he replied with a grin.

Private Fiona McClellan watched the rear approach. Like them, she was under an IR blanket, heat being converted into electricity and discharging slowly into the ground via a lead to a stake. She looked again at her watch; H-Hour minus three. In two hours and fifty-nine minutes, Adkins would put several rounds into the sensor pod. If the submarines had done their job, the orbital approaching would be blinded, giving them a half hour or more window to attack, and destroying the sensor would blind the base defenses.

McClellan thought again about how she had wound up here, sweating her ass off in the cool October sun, rifle in her hands. She had been finishing college, almost ready to become an accountant, when the Invy came, and now she was the mother of one child, with her husband in the actual assault force. Never would have met him if the Invy hadn't come, she mused. Probably never going to see him again if this doesn't work, either.

Adkins was a perpetual complainer, but knew his job well. Though he'd never actually fired on the Invy before, his team regularly hunted the bandits who preyed on small homesteads, in the social anarchy that was once the United Kingdom. Twenty now, he'd known nothing but the occupation, but still resented the life that had been denied him, one that he could barely remember.

Vlonski, well, the Pole hated the Invy with a passion. He had had no communication with his homeland in more than ten years, and didn't know if his wife and children were still alive. What had been a month-long job working on the London docks had turned into eleven years of fighting and killing, and soon, he promised, it would be all over.

"Do you see anything?" he asked Adkins. The younger man had shifted his scope to follow the path of the scout team that was positioning to seize the assault shuttle.

The sniper waited a moment before answering, "I THINK I saw a bit of movement by the port perimeter fence, but I can't be sure. Between those bloody chameleon suits and their skill, I doubt I'd catch anything that might give me a shot. And they're under the blackout cone of the sensor pod tower."

For all his bravery, Vlonski knew that what the scouts were doing took a kind of courage that he didn't have. Each member of the infiltration team was former Special Air Service, Royal Marine Commando, or Special Boat Service. Even more, the two pilots that accompanied them, well, they must have had a serious set of brass balls. To steal an aircraft they had only flown in simulators, with alien controls, fly it nap of the earth, probably under fire, pick up an assault team, and hurtle themselves into space! And yet the CEF commanders and soldiers around him acted as if it were just, as the Americans used to say on TV, a walk in the park.

He looked again at his watch.

H-1:34.

Chapter 42

Warren followed the drones down the corridor, steadily dropping, until they reached the server room. He had no idea what to expect there, but he certainly didn't expect what he did find. Maybe some computers still running, but there was no hum of power, no heat from the banks of machines that filled the room.

"Now what?" he asked out loud, and the drones formed up in front of him, facing the wall. He ran his hand along it, feeling for seams, but there was nothing, until he chanced on a slightly warmer spot on the cool rock face. Closing his eyes, he placed his hand there, and said, as clearly as he could, "*Mellon*", the elvish word for 'friend' from that old movie, then stepped back.

What had seemed to be a solid rock face slowly slid back in the shape a doorway, moving silently, and he stepped forward into the brightly lit room. Inside were banks of monitors, all dark, except for two. One showed a view of the solar system, with several orbital tracks tracing though it, one looping far out towards Persephone and then back inward. The other was a view of Earth, with the Invy orbitals slowly tracing their path around the globe.

He sat in the command chair, a duplicate of the one far above him in the CEF Space Command Center, placed his head into the neural cradle, and waited. Jacking in wasn't always the most pleasant feeling, but now, it seemed almost, well, empty. The entirety of cyberspace, the world within a world, was gone, with its trillion voices all calling to be heard.

After what seemed like an eternity, a figure materialized in front of him. He knew that it wasn't there, merely playing in his optic nerve paths, but still, he wanted to cry. A deep welling of emotion that came from his seventeen-year-old self, the one who had last sat in a chair like this, and talked to his best friend.

"Hal," he whispered.

"David," the projection answered. Like the General, the figure seemed to have aged, to match him. Instead of the teenaged face he had always projected, a near mirror of Warren's own, now there was a mature man, with deep lines of worry and prematurely graying hair. The smile that the AI wore, though, was genuine, an expression of welcome and happiness.

Beside Hal, another figure materialized, less well defined, scratchy, and a bit blurred. It seemed to mirror Kira as Hal mirrored him, as if a fraternal twin. This woman, though, was whole and healthy, not carrying the scars and wasting from the cancer. She was stunningly beautiful, fully grown from the teenager Kira Arkady had been when she went into battle. "Forgive me, General," the AI said, "but I don't have the processing power that I once did, and there hasn't been much light out here in the black."

"Lady Lex. My God," he said, and the tears did come, a great, wracking sob that tore from him. There was hope, after all.

Deep inside Raven Rock, Lieutenant General Dalpe reviewed the plans one more time, knowing that there was nothing he could do to change them. His Main Force units had stealthily converged on the base outside the ruins of Washington, a total of almost a thousand men and women gathered from small units all along the east coast. At H- 00:10, they would attack across cleared fields of fire, aiming to make it to the base operations center. Along with that would come dozens of mortars and heavy machine guns, with some Invy plasma weapons thrown in to boot. For thirty minutes, an eternity in combat, they would attack as hard and as furiously as they could. At H + 00:20, their commander was authorized to withdraw and scatter, or press the attack, as he saw fit.

Major Padilla sat next to him, fingers idly tapping on the table top. Whereas Dalpe was visibly eaten alive by frustration, the Filipino was calm. His role over the last month had been to fine tune the uprising being conducted by the A-Teams. He knew, as did Dalpe, that many of them had no chance of success. A population that was neutral, at best, and a platoon size garrison of Wolverines in each town. Their aim, though, was to cause as much confusion and distraction as possible. If some of them succeeded in defeating the garrisons, well, they would cross that bridge if it was still standing.

The Air Wing CO, Colonel Jameson, had the laid-back attitude of a seasoned fighter pilot, but Dalpe could see the telltale signs of nerves. He wanted to be there, in the cockpit of a Raptor, providing air cover for the two submarines that were sure to come under attack from Invy fighters. His withered legs, though, smashed by the ejection seat of his F-15 during the initial attack, sat strapped to his chair. No, his role had been to train up the pilots on any tactics they could glean from holos of the battles. At H-00:15, the giant hidden steel doors would drop, allowing the air wing to taxi onto the deserted stretch of highway that seemed to end at the mountain, light up their afterburners, and take to the air.

Each was watching the clock, which now displayed H-00:32. Thirty-two minutes until the roll of the dice. If it failed, no one had any illusion that Raven Rock would survive the Invy retaliation.

"Well, I had some hope when Warren showed up, but it died when he disappeared and Kira passed. Really, what do you think our chances are?" asked Jameson.

"Slim to none," answered Dalpe. "The Wolverines are damn good warriors, and for all we know, they might be ready and waiting. It's almost impossible to move a thousand people in twos and threes, and not figure something is up. The Dragons aren't stupid."

All three started when the Ansible console lit up, and a figure started to materialize on the flat projection console. "What the hell?" muttered Dalpe, when the incoming transmission flashed "CEF-SC" instead of "CEF-VL" or "CEF-TD", the two remaining bases with the quantum communication sets.

A miniature representation of General David Warren stood in front of them, with a grin on his face. Behind him were two more figures, one of which Dalpe instantly recognized as Kira Arkady. But she had passed. That meant it was … an AI. The AI of her ship, the carrier *Lexington.* But how?

"Madre de Dios!" breathed Padilla. He had instantly figured it out also.

Jameson was more blunt and to the point, exclaiming, "Holy Shit, that's Hal!"

"Gentlemen, there is little time," said Warren. "Hal has been monitoring Invy communications. In five minutes, the Invy High Command is going to order their forces to high alert. Someone spilled the beans, and we're potentially fucked."

"But ..." The normally talkative Dalpe was at a loss for words. His heart sank down, further than ever before.

Padilla, however, started laughing, and gave a great whoop of joy. "That command isn't going out, is it?"

"No, it's not. Hal has spent the last eleven years infiltrating and decrypting the Invy ansible communications. We still have to deal with the orbitals, but there will be no comms between the Invy cities and their bases. We're going to be on an almost even footing, for as long as Hal can hold them off."

"How long is that going to be?" asked Dalpe, mind running through options. As soon as things kicked off, long hidden radio sets were going to be brought into use, and he would have a battle to fight.

"A half an hour, at most," answered the Artificial Intelligence. "The alien AI are very ... strange, and in many ways do not operate along the same logic lines that I do. I don't expect to survive the encounter, because once I open the pathways of attack, they will be following them back to me."

There was silence for a moment; under the Los Alamos protocol of 2047, Hal and his brothers and sisters had been recognized as fully sentient, living beings. Earth's only other true intelligence, mankind's child, was going willingly to his death to protect them.

"The problem is, General Dalpe," said Warren, "that there are three Invy cruisers in orbit around Titan, where they have a mining operation going. Once the word goes out, those three are going to come screaming in with enough orbital weapons to turn the planet into a cinder. Our ace in the hole is the *Lexington*. If we can catch them with their shields down, damaged as she is, her rail guns might be able to take them out, or disable them. I'm going to need Kira here at the ansible, and Hal has also managed to crack the Invy medical database. There are treatments in there that will have her back …" The excitement in his voice petered out as he saw the looks they gave each other.

"When?" he asked. He was too late.

"A week ago."

Warren's face seemed to crumble in on itself, but then he straightened and let out a long breath. "I can fight the ship from here, with the Lady," he said. Glancing down at his wrist, he finally said, "Gentlemen, in about ten minutes, it's going to be all or nothing. I wish you Godspeed. I'll be here if you need me, but I have a fleet engagement to win."

He saluted, and then the holo flickered out.

Chapter 43

"Colonel, we need those planes up NOW!" said the Raptor pilot.

"Am I talking to Captain Ichijou, or Empress Kiyomi?"

"Both!" she answered, "And it is MY ass, and my pilots, and my subjects, that are depending on you, my Chief of Maintenance. Now I need ten planes, fully armed and fueled in ten minutes!"

The man went away grumbling, and she smiled. Ten was far too many, considering the lack of spare parts and the age of the planes, some almost fifty years old. Six would be enough, based on the scouts' report of Cam Rahm Bay's airfield. She expected four Invy fighters; more would come, but their mission would be over by then. Still, she had to push him.

She climbed the ladder up to her plane, and ran her hand over the five Chinese and two Russian flags painted under her name. The Spratly War had been fought even after the Invy Scout had crashed and the push had been on to form the CEF. She had been just twenty-three, fresh out of the academy, and Japan's first 'Ace' fighter pilot in a hundred years.

As she lowered the cockpit bubble and started the engines, her crew chief gave her a thumbs up; Captain Ichijou returned it. Then he bowed, and fled down the ladder, even as others pulled it away from the rumbling F-22. She looked over and saw the maintenance officer, who held up seven fingers. That would have to do.

The next step on her checklist gave her pause. In place of the 20mm rotary cannon, an Invy anti-tank caliber plasma gun had been retrofitted into her weapons suite. Of course they had never been able to test it on a moving, flying aircraft, but she would have to remember that the muzzle velocity on the weapons rendered the leading of the target negligible.

Ahead, the massive doors concealed in the side of the mountain slowly slid open, revealing the last rays of sunset. She would have preferred the sight of a rising sun, but this would have to do. The pilot slowly increased her thrust, rolling the plane forward, gently working the rudder pedals and brakes to line up with the now wide-open doorway.

When the fighter plane cleared the entrance, she pushed the throttles forward while standing on the brakes. As much as the fighter pilot in her wanted to hit afterburners and rocket down the highway, Kiyomi Ichijou knew that it would be a waste of precious fuel. Instead, once all seven planes of her flight, two F-22s and five of the Japanese version of the venerable F-16, called that they were clear of the doors, she let the brakes go and increased thrust.

The vibration of the engines coursed through her body, and acceleration pushed her back in her seat. She yelled with joy as the front wheels left the ground, and that blissful feeling of being airborne again enveloped her, back in her true element.

Behind her, one of the F-16s suddenly dropped out of the air, several hundred feet off the ground and at several hundred miles per hour. It crashed in a fireball of burning jet fuel, and no chute appeared. Her joy was tempered by their first casualty as she watched it in her rear facing camera, and she said a silent prayer for the man, another good friend.

They quickly flew low over the ocean towards what had been dubbed "Yankee Station", the place where the submarines were to launch, and she wished desperately for an AWACS radar plane to vector them in. Even as they approached, she saw the first series of contrails leaping from the ocean as the missiles reached up for the Invy orbital.

Her call was the only radio traffic to have been heard on Earth in more than a decade. *"For your Empress, for our ancestors, and for us all, let's do this! Sixteen element, stay and cover the submarines. Remember, their interceptors are not really designed for atmosphere. We can out maneuver them. KEEP THEM OFF THE SUBS! Meinu,"* she called to her wingman, *"follow me on high altitude intercept."*

The Raptor leapt upwards, finally set free, almost wingtip to wingtip with her partner. Climbing higher and higher, the sky started to darken before they tipped over and leveled out. She activated the AN/APG-77 radar, giving up the F-22's stealth advantage out of necessity, and immediately got a return, 327 km out, approaching at a closing speed of almost three thousand kph.

"TALLYHO! Six, no, eight Invy approaching at angels 30! Vector 195 degrees, engaging!" The call was for the benefit of the older F-16s, which didn't have the data link the F-22s shared.

Captain Kiyomi Ichijou, set free from the burden of being Empress, dove at the enemy of her world with a fierce, exultant joy in her heart. Even as she did, far to the southwest, another sun blazed forth, and she screamed "BANZAI!!!!" into the radio.

Never mind that it was a nuclear weapon; she had her Rising Sun.

H - 00:03

Chapter 44

"OK, Hal, light it up!" said Warren, and the AI did. Through his neural interface, the room disappeared, and was replaced by a display of the solar system, with orbital tracks of each of the major celestial objects.

One light flashed red, indicating the Invy ships at Titan. Another sparked on and off white, indicating the wormhole junction, far outside the orbit of Neptune. The last icon glowed blue, the position of the *Lexington,* on the same side of the system as Jupiter, but mixed in the asteroid belt.

"Hal, can you access the cruiser's onboard ship systems?"

"No," came the immediate reply. "They are separate from their network on Earth. Given time, yes, but we do not have that time."

There went that idea.

"Lex, give me a status update, quick. Your condition, Invy ship types and capabilities, anything else you think is relevant."

She came back immediately, and he once again thanked the instantaneous communications of the ansible. Without it, a command and response would take minutes. Data began to flow in through his implant, enormous amounts of trajectories, intercept vectors, distances. Weapons capabilities, Invy ship characteristics, weaponry range.

"OK, Lex, give me a visual of yourself. I know it isn't necessary, but please," he asked.

In front of him appeared the blackness of space, with the sun a distant star. The *Lexington* had been designed as a carrier, long and sleek with landing bays extended out on either side, and massive fusion reaction engines in the rear, though they were dead. She looked for all the world like the classic Battlestar, and he wished, for a moment, that they had named her *Galactica.*

Massive solar panels extended out on either side, angled to face the sun; the passive collectors had allowed Lex to remain alive but unnoticed. As soon as the fusion reactors lit up, it would be like setting off a blow torch in a dark room. Even as he watched, they folded inward, and various lights began to glow slightly in the darkness. Their warmth in the coldness of space made his heart beat faster.

Amidships was a massive hole through the body of the ship, and, even after eleven years, there were still bits and pieces of the ship drifting along with her, caught in her slight gravity field. With a start, he noticed that some of the debris were space suited bodies, spinning endlessly in the void. They would be left behind as soon as the *Lex* moved out, but he swore they would be recovered if they won.

"Zoom out," he absentmindedly ordered, falling into command mode. Around the *Lexington* were the shattered remains of her division, the battleships *America,* broken in half, and a debris cloud that was all the was left of the *United States.* All were headed on the same ballistic trajectory they had been on when the battle ended.

"OK, Lex, tell me about your damage. What works, what assets do you have, what can't you do. Give me the bad news first."

"I have full reactor power, in simulation, but I haven't been able to test it. We have devised a gravitic shield similar to the Invy for protection from rail gun rounds, but again only in simulation. Antigravity is, as usual, only adaptable up to five gravities of thrust, but without human crew, I can, in theory, accelerate up to thirty two gravities. Just do not ask me to maneuver at that speed."

"Noted, but that will help. Thirty G's versus the Invy five is going to give us a hell of a tactical advantage."

"This was noted when constructing me, but for some reason, human crews were insisted on."

"Our mistake. What about armament?"

"My mechs have salvaged the main gun of the America, though I cannot guarantee viability. Perhaps a dozen shots. I also have three fighters which are responsive to radio commands. Two are in my hangar bay, one is on a parallel ballistic course approximately three thousand kilometers away. Before his oxygen ran out, the pilot matched speed and course and deployed his solar arrays."

He thought about the man, dying alone, just waiting, and doing one final act of bravery. Damn. Then he considered the guns. That's a 240 mm steel shot accelerated to hypervelocity, he thought. Figure two for each cruiser. It would have to be enough, but those damn shields. The fighters could get inside them, but they would get smoked long before they got close. He also wished for the capability to hit the Invy orbitals with the rail guns, but they would have to save them for space combat.

"What about missiles?"

"I'm sorry," the AI answered, *"but our magazines were expended. Each fighter in my hangar is armed with a three hundred megaton fusion warhead, but I cannot guarantee their functionality."*

"Hal, have either of you managed to come up with anything to defeat their shielding?"

The answer took a minute, which, for an AI, was a lifetime. When he finally answered, it was with a note of resignation. "No, we have not. The only weakness we have found is an approach from the rear. The design of their propulsion requires an opening in the field when they accelerate."

Warren thought hard about what to do. Head to head battle would be a complete disaster; the *Lexington* at her best might have been a match for cruisers, but never capital ships, even with a full complement of fighters to deliver successive bomb pumped x-ray lasers. Now, though…

"David," said Hal, "the submarines have started firing. I must go." With that, Hal's presence disappeared from the net. Warren wished him a silent goodbye, hopefully not for the last time. He looked at the strategic display, and noted the positions of the wormhole, the *Lexington,* and Titan, and sudden inspiration came to him.

"Lex," said General David Warren, "we are going to do some old school Odysseus on the Invy. Put your reactors on standby, juice up the fighters, and start doing some fancy math. I want you to …"

Chapter 45

It was hot, hotter than it should be, but then it always was in a chameleon suit. Nick Agostine sipped slowly at what remained of his water, and watched the Wolverine guard patrol, three of them, slowly following the fence between him and the runway. They were slack, though. Every army has the crappy troops that were regulated to boring guard duty, and it showed here. No joke in a fight, though.

Major Hollister lay there, unseen also. They had left half an hour before Colonel Singh was due to arrive at the hide site, more than three hours ahead of schedule. The pilot knew nothing about the why of moving the time up; she just figured it was part of the plan.

The infiltration had been easier than he expected. Eleven years of occupation without any real fighting had lulled the Invy, or at least the ones at the bases, into a sense of complacency. Their route had been scouted out a week earlier by Reynolds and Zivcovic, all the way up to the airfield fence, taking advantage of every dip in the ground and blind spot on a building.

The whole team was supposed to be there, but Agostine was done with losing those he loved. His family had died in the initial orbital strikes, and over the years, he'd lost teammates on a regular basis. That was why he had kept O'Neill on another team; he never could order her to do something that might result in her death. Now, well, it was all for nothing. She was gone. If the rest of the team survived this mad plan, well, it would ease his conscience a little. Only a little, before he died. He looked at his watch, then raised his rifle, waiting for the roar of fire on the opposite side of the base that signified the diversionary attack, sighting in on the patrol. When the gunfire started, a rolling, muted swell, his eye was already on the sight, red dot on the first creature's head.

Before he could pull the trigger, a muted POP! sounded behind him, and the alien vanished from his sight. His open left eye noted the simultaneous bursts of dark blood from the other two, and he instantly moved, slapping Hollister to get her going, and heading towards the runway. He hadn't made it more than twenty feet when he heard the whine of an APC roaring down the runway. The Quick Reaction Force had moved faster than he thought they would. Behind him, Sergeant Zivcovic gave his distinctive yell of

"URRAH!" and, though he knew they would all soon be dead, he was suddenly glad that they would be with him in the end. A Javelin anti-tank missile leapt from under an IR blanket, rocketed forward, popped up, and then detonated directly over the APC, causing it to burst into flames and skid across the concrete.

"TAKE THAT, MOTHERFUCKERS!" yelled Boyd, as he and Hamilton worked feverishly to load another round on the targeting unit. With practiced speed, Boyd launched another rocket at the airfield barracks, this one a thermobaric warhead designed to detonate inside the building. With a WHOOMP of displaced air, it exploded, blowing out every window in the building and setting a raging fire.

Agostine grabbed Major Hollister by the arm and ran her forward toward the target ship. Looking over, he saw Jonesy, concealing hood thrown back, grabbing her other arm. The two of them practically carried the pilot to the ship, her boots barely touching the ground. "I'm ... going... to... have... you ... all ... shot!" grunted Agostine under the weight of his pack, rifle, and the Major. Jones just laughed and ran harder as plasma bolts started to kick up dirt around them.

Looking out of the hatch of the ship was an Octo; it was the reason they had chosen this ship, knowing that they ran pre-dawn checks on each, and this would be the first. It disappeared in a purple spray as a shot from Reynolds knocked it backward.

As the two of them almost hurled the Major into the open hatchway, the Master Sergeant yelled to her, "GO! GET THE HELL OUT OF HERE!" and threw himself down on the concrete, sighting on the approaching dismounted Wolverines. He felt the rest of the team fall in around him as the engines started to spool up; they began directing their fire at the heavier weapon emplacements around the airfield, suppressing the surprised crews. One operating heavy plasma gun could easily turn the assault shuttle into shredded metal. Unsuppressed weapons, rifles and machine guns long hidden, barked out their song, and Agostine felt the call of battle roar in his ears with a fierce joy.

He thought, about how Brit would have loved to see this day, and wished for some bagpipes to accompany their fight. The music unnerved the Wolverines, and he remember their effect at the battle of Cheyenne Mountain. Then, over the gunfire, he did hear them, faint on the wind; the swirl of pipes as someone from the Main Force attack lit into "Scotland the Brave", and he smiled, looking down the line at men and women fighting beside him. Past them smiled back the ghost of a beautiful red haired woman, sky blue eyes blazing brightly.

"Live!" she said, and then vanished in the light of very red, very bloody dawn.

The Beginning...

Appendix 1

CEF Rank Structure:

Enlisted

Private (PVT)

Private First Class (PFC)

Corporal (CPL)

Staff Sergeant (SSG)

Sergeant First Class (SFC)

Master Sergeant (MSG)

Sergeant Major (SGM)

Officer

Second Lieutenant

First Lieutenant

Captain

Major

Lieutenant Colonel

Colonel

Brigadier General

Major General

Lieutenant General

General